GREAT AMERICA IN DEAD WORLD

DAVID AGRANOFF

First Edition

Cover Image by Keith Giles
Cover Design and Interior Layout by Matthew J. Distefano

Print ISBN: 978-1-964252-46-9
Electronic ISBN: 978-1-964252-47-6

Published by Quoir
Chico, California
www.quoir.com

1

The parts of Kai that were not human were already awake when her alarm went off. She opened her eyes slowly and saw the blinking notifications in the bottom right of her vision. Her membership to the Dream Circuit had expired at midnight. She had a vague memory of a dream she hadn't paid for. There was an ad for a radio show by a political commentator, Steve O'Connell: "You will never forget those, they are just beyond your psyche like an echo."

The natural dreams, as always, were nonsensical and frustrating. They were about work, but she could barely remember it as she looked up at the ceiling. At this time of year, there was an orange glow in the morning; her window faced the east. When she was younger, the sun would've blinded her natural eyes as she sat up, but the smog dulled them now.

Good morning, Kai. Her avatar texted on her slide. It glowed on the night-stand by her bed.

"Prepare sync," whispered Kai. It was the first thing she did in the morning. See what her Aver did when she gave up control. She hated letting the program play the game for her, but *Night Warrior* had four hundred and twenty levels of gameplay, and players around the globe constantly. The game never stopped, and players who slept were constantly getting knocked below 200-level, which meant you didn't even earn coins. The competition was fierce.

Twenty-seven confirmed kills, 4 identity suits claimed, 13 levels advanced, and 48 coins earned.

Kai felt she could have done better but it was a decent night of play. The idea was that you trained the program with your habits, and it could move faster than a natural mind. Kai hadn't had an unaltered brain since she was a child. Most augments were about survival, even those about operating the net, grid, or Sims. She looked in on the live feed. The game led her into a concert hall. A virtual crowd was forming, and there were reports of mass shooters in the building. It was no different than the real world; you had to pay attention to the forecast. It was the only way to be sure. She pulled up live market rates from the exchange, one hundred coins for a kill or capture. She cracked her knuckles, ready to hunt.

"Sync and give me ammunition and weapon levels."

In the game, she lifted her rifle and scanned for the shooter as she approached the elevator. She pushed the button and waited.

"Miss Kai, I am sorry to be the one to remind you that your shift begins in less than two hours.

Her bed spoke with the insistence of a device designed for impatience. She had registered it for no more than 230 pounds, and a six-hour sleep cycle. She had to pay for each minute she went overtime and the pound of pressure she put on the smart coils. She was not a tall woman, but her augments put her over the weight limit. An ad for drought-resistant Calgary almond-based Foodle flicked across her blanket. Until she paid up she would have to endure the pop-ups from her total sleep unit. Once the ten-second point passed, she wiped it away.

Go to work, I've got this. In the last couple of months, her avatar texted this type of thing more often.

Kai noticed the "*I*" statement. The avatar was supposed to maintain her social media and game engagement as she slept or was busy at work. It was the first bill she paid every month or else her Manager was useless. It wasn't an *I*. Some people thought of their Avers as alive or friends who were separated from them but that just wasn't the case.

She looked at the glowing device at her bedside. The Manager was five inches tall and three across. It was thicker than glass and operated all her systems, biological, mechanical, and virtual. She received thirty notifications from past-due bills and ads for ways to spend her coins inside the game. When she went to bed, they were down to four coins.

The concert started inside the game. A kid's show with giant mascots. A big red dinosaur danced on the stage. The concert was filled with children and families. Not real ones, but that explained why the coins they could earn were off the charts. Shooters who targeted children were valuable. Kai selected enter and the number fifty came up in a notification from the game admin. Fifty coins just to get in. That was close to everything she had.

Go to work. Another text.

Kai felt like her own program was annoyed with her. She knew she had to go to work. One day of work in the real world meant they could transfer funds for serious coin. She needed to check the exchange rate. If they could get to 300 hundred level, play the game for work, or even afford GA+ membership, then she could hire the other jackass at work to be her Janie.

We can get a few kills on this level.

It said *we* this time. Avers, the good ones, can read their hosts' minds--not telepathically, but predictively. She'd loaded the program herself using all the personal data she'd input to her Manager since her mother had given her the unit. The government provided payment programs for Manager slides as they were essential to maintain their great simulation. The Manager was essential for daily life for people who couldn't afford Prime or Plus membership.

She put her feet on the floor and felt the carpet beneath her toes. Kai pushed the control button and selected slide control. "Can I get the forecast?"

Avers, avatars, or cloner programs are not supposed to be alive, just be the AI that runs your personal slide Manager, what old people called their phones fifty years ago. Hers preferred they or it, as a working pronoun, but Kai had friends whose Avers picked genders. Why that mattered for a computer program, she couldn't say. It seemed like a liberal notion of the elites she couldn't understand. She was told gender mattered in GA+, but she hadn't spent more than a few minutes in the Sim during her whole life.

Stepping into the bathroom mirror, she cringed, expecting to see a funky bedhead. Her hair, styled in a short pixie, was dyed dark red at the roots and blue, green, and purple at the tips. Her bright diamond blue eyes were her most expensive feature; her interface reflected against her inner eye, and optical Sim control was not cheap. It was not just tech crossovers. Her eyes also must survive intense heat and dust storms, which were all too common in LA these days. It was a ritual for her to look at herself for a long time in the mirror before getting dressed.

The forecast scrolled along the bottom of the mirror. *"Presented by LA group injury attorneys. High of 115 degrees with a heat index of 125. Forty-six percent chance of afternoon Santa Ana dust storms. There is a 35% chance of mass public shootings. *Click here for self-defense upgrades.* Sunset at eight p.m. with orange contrails all along the way."*

Kai slid off her pants and used her slide to select an outfit. Her Aver sent a list of the next available sky trams she could catch. There was one coming to the building roof-port in five minutes.

"I can't, I need the next one." Kai sat on the toilet and instantly felt more comfortable as she peed. She had enough of her original parts to still have a bladder. She had to drink less water thanks to her new skin and coolant tattoos. It was the thing that made it harder to pass. Her skin didn't burn, but she sprayed on protection all the same. She was still peeing, and even though the Aver didn't say anything she had a sense that her program was annoyed by this basic human function. Kai ran into the bedroom and found her new outfit waiting on the bed as the closet closed itself.

"I will get to work when I can," she said aloud as her slide transmitted her voice to all her devices. "I need a bottle of Foodle to go." Her contact lens displayed her current Foodle stock. She had breakfast and lunch bottles but would have to mix the powder packs when she got home.

The arms from the fridge placed the two bottles just off her path so she could sweep them off the counter into her shoulder bag. All of her systems were working to get her on the first Skytram. The difference in salary for a full day was motivation enough. All programs reacted to her desires, as a good AI learned to do.

———

The temperature rose steadily in the morning and was north of one hundred on the surface by eight in the morning. The low temperature never got below ninety-five degrees Fahrenheit in Los Angeles at this point. It was the reason why the Skytrams were created; most buildings and the most expensive real estate on the West Coast rose over the heat domes. Kai couldn't imagine living in a building that didn't have a rooftop port. A westbound tram was not due for three minutes when she walked on the roof. George stood in the shade with his Manager in his hand. He was in a suit, his tie loosened, sweat already intense and dripping on his brow.

"Morning Georgie," Kai smiled and waved her half-consumed Foodle bottle.

He smiled at her, as he always did. He worked at the court downtown and was getting close to enough money for a GA + membership. His mood went from constant frustration at the heat and dust storms to jovial humor over the last few weeks. People got that way when a great change was in sight.

"Morning Kai, who did your hair... Crayola?" He smiled as if he said something hilarious, but Kai didn't get the joke. He was thirty years older and his humor sometimes made sense for a world that she never experienced. She smiled and pointed at her new do as if she got the joke. He shrugged and she assumed that he was fine if she didn't get the joke.

Her mind was a million other places: money, the apartment, the sleep unit, her Manager, and, of course, the game. She just wanted to be playing *Warrior*.

"Careful out there today," George didn't look up his slide. Working for the city, he did have some information that was not on the slides.

She pulled hers out of her pocket and opened each of her social platforms and news apps. She had a system that took about thirty seconds; she could open all other main apps scroll quickly and look for a topic and if anything was there, she could find it. Nothing on Town Square, Neighborhub, or Socials. Instaspace, Friendline, Yearbook, and Videoport were all trending with GA + internal gossip.

"What am I looking for Georgie?"

"Didn't hear it from me?" That was a question, and she nodded. They had gone through this before. She had not betrayed his trust. She was very careful what she posted in general, but George let city business slip all the time. She smiled at him. He was a sucker for her smile and carefully chosen head tilts. She watched his judgment.

"Okay. Foodle riots over in Studio City. There were no shipments of actual food."

Kai rolled her eyes. "What is so bad about Foodle? It is food."

"That's a young person talking. My boy Alexi plays *Citizen Savior and Night Warrior*. He lives on GA+, I haven't seen anything but his feet in months. He plays live in four windows, and he programmed Avers so he could play under four user names at once. Foodle was fine for him as long he was not hungry. Foodle is just protein, and vitamins, but food..."

She didn't want a back-in-the-day lecture and leaned over the edge of the building hoping to see the Skytram due any minute.

"Kai, let me ask you something?"

The hovering Skytram turned the corner with a woosh as it pulled up to the port.

"My ride is here," She pointed at the tram, even though she knew George was boarding too. She hoped he got the idea she wasn't in the mood. "Speaking of *Warrior*, I am running a campaign myself...."

"Have you had a banana?"

She was confused. "Excuse me? Hold on, Georgie. It is not like you're not getting a GA+ membership, I know..."

"Have you ever eaten a banana?"

Eaten. So, it was a food of some kind. She looked at her slide. He reached out and put his hand over the screen.

"You were going to look it up." George shook his head.

"No, no. It is food, a..." She snapped her fingers.

"A fruit," George said as the door to the tram opened. "A delicious fruit. My grandma called it nature's candy bar."

A hologram advertising a banana-flavored foodie popped up in the space between them.

"Sorry," Kai swiped the ad away. It was embarrassing that she had no money to turn off floater ads.

It was George's turn to roll his eyes as the tram door opened behind them. The people getting on and off didn't look at each other and seemed to run into each other. Kai sees it every workday. It is like the people getting on and off don't consider that anyone exists or might be using the same tram. There is a confused dance as each one figures out how to get past the others.

"Young people," George muttered. "Learn to live in the world, please!" he pushed his way into the car. The tram was twenty-five years old, and while in service that whole time, the plastic seats were cracked and dust damaged. They hurt your ass if you sat too long. During rush hour, it was mostly workers, plenty of Janies, and advertisements that popped up around the tram. Foodle drinks, employment agencies, lawyers, and GA+ memberships, the floaters targeted your Manager and would follow you if you tried to walk away. The ads crowded the space when gamers concentrated and didn't swipe. They caught the eyes of those looking and adapted to your interests. Her eye augments caught the swipes, so she saw them anyway. She needed to pay up or the pop-up chasers would follow her all day.

Kai sat down and opened her slide. Her avatar was in the middle of a battle with a mass shooter. The Aver had spent her coin, to get into the concert hall and confront the shooter. She looked at the game controller and saw three other living players. Kai employed a VPN to make it appear as a living player even with her Aver. You never really knew, as the program could speak in the user's voice. She pressed her earlobe, and the implant played the sounds of the scene before her view opened. Shots fired, screams of children.

"Engage sync."

The Manager opened her first-person POV, and she lay on the ground as a bullet whizzed above. Concert shooters were worth serious coin, child killers even more. She had five minutes before her tram stop to play the game live. She closed her eyes; she was going fully into the game.

The sound of the screams and bullets felt extreme; once the shooting began, the player without experience would run, afraid that their Avers would die. It is expensive to resurrect an avatar in the game, but many forget your Aver only dies inside the game. Remembering that helps one to play with a little bit more Once you earn 200 level points you can buy armor. It would cost fifty coins, but if she bagged this shooter, they would profit by one hundred and fifty coins.

It had to be a night shooting. She scrolled the database, using a snapshot of the room to try and identify the real-life incident. The game accessed the historical details of over 100,000 available nighttime mass shooter events from the United States and Great American databases. The source record quickly matched a 2017 event, gunfire at the Sesame Kids live concert in Kansas City. That would explain the screaming children. Records indicate a lone wolf with Daddy issues, two legally bought AR-15s, sixty-five rounds, and twenty-two victims. She looked at the current score of five dead; she still had seven teenage victims to save, and she only needed to save ten to win the simulation.

Kai's avatar in the game used an operating suit and looked more like a 20th-century action movie hero, with skin painted blue and white. They moved along the floor as the first blasted above. Another player with a virtual suit was moving along the floor, and it was a race to the center aisle of the theater. She did a quick search of the player's IP. Snatch_22 was a popular gamer who streamed his play with millions of viewers who tried and failed to copy his strategies. There would be many eyes on this game if she had more coin left and could put up a "follow me" flag.

The shooter stayed on the stage, firing what seemed like endless bullets. Kai controlled the interface on the slide, never opening her eyes. Seeing the tram around her would break her focus. She could see Snatch, who had a smaller, faster avatar, reaching the center aisle first. Using expensive upgrades, his avatar slid under and through the seat, changing shape to fit and slithering like a snake. He spent serious coin for that kind of hero suit.

With nothing she could do but watch, the Avatar stood up shirtless, covered in camo-painted muscles as it shot a barrage of machine gun fire.

"Shit," Kai opened her eyes and unsynced her avatar. She hated losing, and later, she might pull up the stream.

She looked across the tram. George was reading something on his slide. He read articles, like a boring old person.

⁕

Kai stepped off the tram at the Skyport building. Two other Janies came off the tram, carrying their tool cases; it was the clearest sign of their occupation. Kai wore hers in a shoulder bag. It was heavier, but she was less obvious walking around. Hackers sometimes followed well-paid Janies back to their client's homes. She carried disinfectant, disposable wipes, and tools. The client was expected to provide their own Foodle. Deliveries sometimes were waiting at the door or up here on the roof. She didn't see anything and hoped these people had what they needed. She swiped away ads for apartments and nightclubs, they followed her as she walked, and every tenth ad couldn't be swiped. She tuned out as the ad for a new Sim called '*Heaven for the Living.*'

"Experience your last heatwave with Heaven for the Living. A realistic life Sim for up to twenty members interested in living

forever in a world tailored to their loves and joys. Heaven is more than a promise now—it is a membership you can afford."

The building had a neon sign that was cursive, and the glow cut through gritty air. The Waverleigh's name glowed in neon, but written under it in chipped paint "21st century Conapts—condominium conversion pods for the Great American lifestyle." The other Janies were having a conversation, and they seemed familiar to each other. The building knew their faces and let them in, but this was a new client for Kai. The door locked on her. She reached twice, but she heard the lock catch. She pulled out her Manager to text the building's operating system.

Janitorial and pod maintenance for the Runcibles in Apt 355. Requesting access.

The door snapped open, and Kai looked up to the camera inside the door. "Can you put my face ID on file please?" Buildings hardly respond so she walked to the lift. The air conditioner kicked on stronger as she dropped the seventeen floors. When she stepped into the third-floor hall she saw one of the Janies from the roof going into another apartment. A door opened down the hall. She knew it was 55. She walked toward it and could hear the AC working to cool the space. The pod units regulated their body temperatures, and the AC only came on if the residents were awake or had visitors.

The hallway was like an oven, funked up by humidity just three levels from the surface. Kai waited outside as the AC regulated the temperature inside and coughed the stagnant air out. She felt the cooling elements under her tattoos cool her skin. The hall would be unbearable without them. As the door opened and Kai walked into the air-conditioned room, she wondered how Arnold and Janet Runcible made their coin. The apartment was not much bigger than their pods which breathed as loudly as an iron lung. Inside the room, the bodies of the couple lived on so their minds could enjoy the benefits of all that hard work.

On the wall were several photos of the couple playing tennis; a square-jawed athletic man and a well-dressed slightly younger woman. They had more pictures of tennis rackets than of their two kids. Most of the pictures had been chosen to show off their athletic nature. A photo had been placed prominently on the desk—Janet, who'd once been an important woman, had been staged in an awkward photo with the President Supreme when he was still doing public rallies.

Walking further into the apartment, Kai realized this job would be more than simple cleaning. His and hers pods were in rough shape. She walked along the pod and looked to see what she was dealing with. The Foodle ports were crusted with molding green junk, the air vents were covered in dust slowly becoming goop. She pulled the covers off the hands and feet, the nails that had grown into curls.

This was Janie malpractice.

Her slide lit up with a notification. *Janet Runcible has sent you a GA+ chat invite.*

She would have to pause her Aver, to reroute the bandwidth and log into the guest network. The program would argue with her if she didn't do it quickly. It was best to lie down if you didn't have a pod for the interface. She was a guest, and not fully integrated so the Sim would not be as life-like as it would be for a real member. Kai lay on the floor feeling the carpet against her back as she hit the link to log in.

Wait, no let me keep playing...

Reality folded in for a moment. It felt a little like stepping off a diving board, not that Kai ever had that experience. She just knew it felt like falling. The apartment faded away. The words floated around her and came into being for a moment before her...

GREAT AMERICA PLUS GUEST MEMBERSHIP LOADING

The words faded into a fine mist, leaving her in another world. The first thing she noticed was the blue sky, clear except for a few wispy clouds. The air neither hot nor humid. She moved her hand around in the air, and it felt thin. A breeze came across her face. Her mind was convinced it was a breeze. The view was the coastline, might have been California but she understood Great American geography was different. Waves crashed into the source with a gentle rhythm. This felt very real, and a guest membership was only a fraction of the realism promised to 'paying' members.

She selected her work agency avatar that looked like her, with shoulder-length brown hair and her natural face.

"Stay chill," she whispered to herself. Already she wanted to be here, to live here, in this world. Every time she had been here it only lasted minutes and she always wanted more. Her father had loved to remind her it wasn't real. Maybe not, but it was nice. What was real anyway?

Kai spun and saw a tennis club. Arnold Runcible sat in a chair off the tennis court, looking over the ocean. Next to him was Janet who appeared to be ten years younger than the pictures in the apartment. She'd spent money programming her avatar. Her legs were muscled, her face free of wrinkles, and the light freckles Kai had thought were so cute in the pictures were gone. Kai had to fight an urge to reach up and touch the ultra-smooth skin of the woman's face. Arnold had lost the spare tire, and he no longer bore the thick body hair he had in the pictures. They were living commercial for the lifestyle in Great America-Plus.

Kai approached, getting used to walking in the Sim.

"Welcome, Miss." Janet sat next to her husband.

"Kai, my name is Kai Dame, just call me Kai."

"Welcome." Arnold smiled. "We just have a few things to go through."

"It is a beautiful Sim you have here."

"It is not ours, I'm afraid. We are just logged in like most Americans."

The ones with money, Kai thought to herself.

"We pay for it. Hopefully, one day we will be able to pay for something a little more private."

She shot a dirty look at the mother and daughter playing tennis a few courts down. The mother and daughter were logged into the same club. They were real avatars, not digitally simulated phantoms. The GA+ control unit sometimes filled in simulations to give the population a fuller look.

Speaking of payments," Kai said, smiling, "I understand you are new to Friendlies pod maintenance; we have top-of-the-line service."

"How bad is it? We have not logged out in some time."

"Yeah, I could tell."

Arnold sighed, but Janet stiffened, her smooth forehead creasing into a frown.

"Who was your last contract with?" Kai thought she knew, but she needed to ask.

"Aja's Domestics."

"His shop is not union, and it shows."

"We learned our lesson, no need to shame us," Janet sighed, her frown remaining.

Aja undercut the prices of union shops but relied on subs and temp workers he could pay off the books in cash and not pay for insurance. The program glitched for just an instant, an accidental reminder that she was a guest there.

"How bad is it?" Arnold took a drink and fooled his mind that he was hydrating with something besides Foodle.

"Pretty bad," Kai said. "I have to do some grooming on top of setting up a long-term Foodle drip to keep nutritional needs going."

Janet cringed a bit: she had vanity still about her real-world body. Kai could tell Arnold didn't care about vanity. They were not as thankful to her as some clients. Many of these rich fucks forget that Janies keep them alive. Still, these assholes would earn her the coin she needed.

"My husband doesn't give a shit, but I do. Please make sure we are presentable."

"I never log out anymore; I work from here, " he said casually, obviously not thinking about how privileged he sounded.

Kai wanted to enjoy the breeze, but she knew they would lock her out soon; she had to feed these helpless fucks. In the corner of her vision, her Manager offered up three response options, but the company slogan was blinking; her Manager clearly wanted her to select it. She could almost hear her company training videos. *Be reassuring; they trust their earthly bodies to take your care.*

"I got you; your job is just to relax." She repeated the Friendlies pod maintenance slogan under their logo and the signature on their e-mails. "Your job is to relax."

Kai logged out, and the Conapt came back to life around her. Even in the AC, the air felt warm and soupy. She looked at Janet Runicble's curled toenails. She had work to do.

2

THE BREEZE WAS PERFECT, as it was every day. The morning sky was always blue, the grass damp with dew, and the ground was drying out. It had rained overnight as it always did in Great America. It was always cook-out weather here, and many people used their avers to work so finding cook-outs and other social engagements was an easy way to fill your calendar.

Miranda Greenstone walked out onto the porch. She was a perfect vision of the woman he had married decades ago. His favorite green dress hugged a flawless hourglass figure. They had updated their programs with expensive algorithms that let them pick the image of the spouse of their choice. Miranda might have had a different vision of herself.

Roger Greenstone had ten photographs of his wife, all from their courtship and newlywed years. The picture of her in the green dress was from their engagement party, the day they sneaked out to the bathroom and conceived their oldest daughter—at least they *think* that was when it happened. That was sexy young Miranda, and she likely now saw him as the thinner, dark-haired, rising political operative she'd met when they were in their last year at Yale.

She handed him a drink as he gazed at the ocean rolling into the shore of Martha's Vinyard, or at least the GA+ version. Virtual real estate, in this case, was just as expensive as the real thing. He sniffed the drink.

"Whiskey? A little early."

"You turned off your notifications. I thought you would need one before you looked at them."

"Shit, just tell me."

He glanced at her. She was the woman he married in every sense, even if their aging bodies lay next to each other in the pods. He watched the drink move as he shook the glass slightly. Even after all these years, the details always amazed him.

"DC, today."

"Washington? I can log into the White House server..." She shook her head. He sipped the whiskey again. "Fuck, he wants me really there. Why?"

"Physical hours are billable; he must have reason."

"It is not his money; he loves spending everyone else's money."

She put a finger in front of her perfectly red lips. Roger didn't care. He knew where decades of bodies were buried. More importantly, he knew the biological nature of many on the staff at the White House. The evangelical base had supported him from the start, even when he was cheating on his pregnant wife and mocking the disabled on stage. His hypocrisy was a marketable part of his brand when his base chose to believe whatever they liked. It was true that President Supreme supported the court when they declared that people with more than 50% technological augments were non-humans. The 50-plusers had no rights—they were legally more machine than human.

The darker truth the public didn't know but could easily guess was that all these decades later, the cabinet was filled with 50-Plusers who would have died of old age and natural causes long ago. The amount of time they spent living in the Great America Plus Sim was the legal loophole, as they had separate rights in Great America Plus, rights that the 50-P in the real world didn't need. They skirted term limits to be in the government the same way, the billable physical time was all that counted toward their term limits.

"It is good timing; I needed you to talk to my father."

His father had a GA+ membership he and his wife had given him, and he used it, but mostly to visit them. He was a Luddite who chose to live with the dust storms and heatwaves.

"I talked to him a week ago, at the cookout after Scotty's baseball game."

"He hasn't logged in since, and you know why."

Roger was just weeks from retirement when that happened. By then they would have the money and path to a personal Heaven server. If they were going to stay together as a family, they had to enter the Sim together. The brain box had to integrate all the brain patterns together as it built your personal simulation, or "Heaven," according to the marketing.

"Miranda, He is making a choice."

"He is coming with us, or..."

She didn't have to say it. She wouldn't go without him. He was a tough old bastard, but she loved him deeply. After Yale, he had followed her home, he was elected to Congress in a rare at the time republican district in southern Orange County, California. They worked hard to get out, everyone but her father. She expected him to return to the West Coast and talk to her father. Roger had not spent more than a few hours in the real world for a decade now.

"Baby, you can't expect...uh, that could take days," he fumbled the words.

She gave him a look that only this version of her could pull off. It was a pouty, but pretty look. He had no choice but to get her father to understand. The logistics were the thing he was struggling with. She understood the look was not overruling the planning he was doing in his head.

"I have a new service." Roger rubbed his temple. "Higher-quality, top-of-the-line Janies. They will be there to work with you."

She shrugged. "You're the Chief of Staff; the PS is not using Air Force One."

"I'll have to fly commercial, the Air Force flies only drones now."

She reached forward and caressed the back of his neck. She leaned in and kissed him. She smelled like roses, and her lipstick was programmed to give him extra tingles. She held his lower lip between hers, and he felt the arousal to his toes.

"Come home quick. I have a surprise for you. I know they will give your Air Force Four."

"That was naughty, Mandy," he whispered. She smiled at the name he used only in their sweetest moments.

She let his lip go, and he watched her slink back into the house. He thought he saw the program glitch. A skip. He worried sometimes that she had built an avatar to manipulate him and was somewhere living another program. Some of the guys at the office were doing that. It could be done if you had enough bandwidth, but it was hard on the brain. He couldn't risk it. He had too many responsibilities at work.

The kiss echoed in his mind. He had to get back here as quickly as possible. Words floated in his vision.

YOUR APPOINTMENT IS IN FIVE MINUTES.

It was disorienting. When you spend months or years fooling your mind, it accepts the Sim more and more. GA+ is his mind's world.

The program is designed to make your brain feel everything your real body would feel and then some. The actual smell is the first thing you sense, and no matter how well-paid and hard-working your Janies are, they only clean the tubes coming in or out so much. Roger pulled the Foodle nodes out of his nose with a snap. The smell of the paste is terrible, but sadly, you get used to it. The icky feeling of humid air and real smells without filters was the worst. He couldn't stand the thought that for the majority of human existence, the body and all its horrors were a fact of life.

The worst indignity is waiting for the Janie who is supposed to pull them out of your ass. The tubes are caked with months of waste, and even though the Foodle drips send cleaning fluids through weekly, there is only so much it can clean. His penis was not erect, but that sometimes made it easier for extracting the waste tube.

The Janie was a young man he had never seen before. He put away his slide Manager, and as he moved closer, Roger looked through hazy goop,

goop-covered eyes. The Janie had on a DC friendlies uniform, and Roger got a look at the name tag—Holden, just as the young man grasped his penis and gently pulled the tube free. He tapped it with his right hand to make sure no urine was caught in it.

He lifted Roger with the ease of a person with augmented arms. His hands were cold to the touch, perhaps robotic. Roger preferred indentured cyborgs because they didn't have union rights even when they worked for unionized companies.

The tube came out of his ass, and Roger tried to prop himself up.

Holden held his ass tube and said his opening line according to his company script. "Welcome home, Mister Greenstone."

Roger waved him off. "Please rinse that foul thing out." He looked around the small apartment as Holden disappeared into the bathroom and ran the water in the tub. Sitting up, he could see out his thirty-sixth-floor window. The Washington Monument didn't sway, but everything in the DC skyline was in chaos. From high above Silver Spring, he could watch the angry weather that rolled off the hot waters of the Atlantic. The new weather pattern sent tropical storms and hurricanes down on the capital for the summer and early fall months. It looked like they were in a lull between storms.

D.C. was now a series of Islands that housed important buildings. There had been an attempt to market it as the Venice of America, but it was impossible. The wind gusts and humid rains were the temperature of bath water.

His slide Manager sent the forecast to his contacts, and it appeared in the corner of his vision. There is a 76% chance of rain and heavy winds. Tracking shows tropical depression Gina hitting in twelve hours with 120 MPH winds.

"The White House is sending an Auto." Holden came out of the bathroom with a clean, clear tube. "I assume they are shooting to finish your meeting before the storm." Holden smiled. He was probably 60% technology and 40% biological. In reality, he was more human than Roger himself. The difference was that his implants and augments were designed to hide his nature as a member of the President Supreme's staff; he had to uphold a certain natural image. Many of their base considered anyone with more than 50% technology to be insulting to the holy spirit.

Roger eyed his nearly naked body in the window's reflection. Rounder, softer, with almost no hair left that was not generated by augments. A man his age would be dead or infirm long ago. He took a moment to look at Miranda's pod. He could see her puffy, ancient, veiny hands.

Holden handed him a bottle of Foodle Awake, and he drank it as fast as he could get it down.

He needed a shower. Gravity was a feeling people in the real world took for granted. As he walked to his clothes, he felt like he was dragging an anchor outside the Sim. Holden was shameless, and Janies were here to serve. Holden had a damp washcloth and was already rinsing Roger's arms. He continued to stare at his own reflection. It took time for his mind to accept reality. He gripped the air to work out his mechanical parts.

He had just enough technology to keep him functioning into his eighties with the energy he needed for the job, and to survive the extreme conditions. The last years of the 21st century were a consequence of actions they argued were a hoax for decades. He thought about the simulation he left behind, the one promise the President Supreme made and kept. Great America Plus.

The Auto-Auto didn't need wipers, the driving function was programmed, and the car didn't care if he could see the capital city as they drove through the pouring rain. He trusted that it. As they hit the flood zone, the wheels folded in, and they floated straight into the tube that tunneled under the last three blocks before the White House. In his first term, President Supreme hated this building, called it a dump, and did everything he could to be at his golf courses. Now those golf courses were nothing more than a state of mind. After he fought so hard to get back here, he never again wanted to leave.

The White House had become an obsession; The President Supreme could've been further north, away from the storms, but he had both of the

First Ladies' pods, and his own, just off the Oval Office in the president's quarters. His body had not left the building in decades outside of logging into GA + where he had held his rallies for years now. In the Sim, he could raise Old Glory with his mind and shoot bald eagles out of his fingertips, just like his followers always believed he could.

A red scan hit his right eye, and he relaxed a little knowing his clearance was being accepted. When the car stopped in the muggy basement garage, the AC could only do so much as he stepped out in time to see the secretary of state and the PS's young grandson getting out of his Auto.

"Roger Greenstone," Jared Hewitt said, grinning. Jared was an asshole's idea of a fuckface. "Well, can we still call you Roger? I mean, how much of you is Artiforgs at this point? I mean, you gotta be rocking some serious tech." He shook Roger's hand with an over-the-top grip, maybe artificial.

Glass houses. Roger thought about saying it.

"Doctor Hewitt." Roger nodded. The thirty-two-year-old nitwit got an honorary doctorate from Wabash College. He insisted they call him "Doctor" instead of Secretary of State; an honorary figurehead position and an excuse for a free lifetime login for GA Plus.

"Any idea why the boss wanted us?"

"If we are both here it is a matter of foreign relations."

"Oh god, why do we still have to deal with other countries...."

"We hardly do anymore."

Hewitt made finger guns and stuck out his tongue. "You're welcome."

They got in the elevator. The gold walls shone far too bright for his eyes, which had gone months unused. The music was a compilation of the songs they played at rallies in the early days—patriotic ballads mostly, but there was nothing worse than getting trapped in the elevator with the boss when the Village People or Ave Maria came on. He did a dance and wanted his staff to tell him what a great dance it was. If you stayed silent, you would get a dirty look.

They got off in the Oval Office and looked around. The President gazed out the large windows, the gears and wires that maintained his joints purred and whined as he turned to push his Diet Coke® button. One factory in New Jersey supplied the kitchen, and no one had the heart to tell the boss that sugar in his soda was a Foodle blend, but after they returned to the White House they reinstalled the famous Diet Coke® button, it was a day one priority.

Roger did enjoy watching the bravado drain out of Hewitt as he stepped into this office; everywhere else in the world (or in the Sim), he was king shit of turd mountain. The President was aware of what a colossal asshole his grandson was, and as it always was with two unmovable objects the collusion was amusing to watch. Roger had worked with President Supreme during all the ups and downs. He was the greatest sore loser the human race had ever known, but God blessed them both for his stubbornness; he was a sore loser but also a comeback kid who refused to be down.

He always won now; it was the law. It was ironclad, part of the fabric of the nation at this point.

"Mister President, you are looking well." Hewitt might as well have kissed his cottage cheese-like behind, but that was part of the job. Roger didn't bother with small talk. The President's comb-over was a sculpture when he was still human, now it was nothing short of orange Elvis. If you are what you eat, the last living parts of his body were a product of the few remaining farms kept for domestic animals as stock. His mechanical legs worked harder each year to support the living parts of his body; his heart had been replaced three times, and his skin, hair, and mind were all that remained natural, things he insisted on. Donated parts cloned and replaced were technically his. All his vanity existed with his loving supporters in the Sim. He didn't give a fuck what the rest thought of him. They were losers who couldn't afford his greatest achievement. In the Sim, he looked like his supporters thought of him. Chiseled, strong, and designed to look the part of a President.

"Mister President, I was wondering why you needed us here..."

"I bet you are Greenstone. I bet you are."

Roger waited. He would use his first name if he was getting beat up on social media.

"They are saying bad things, Roger, very bad things."

"Who, sir? Who is saying bad things?"

"Oh, come on, they are."

His poll numbers in GA+ were above 80%. Unheard of when he was in office the first time, before the second revolution. As the human race had to adapt to the rising temperatures, living more and more in virtual reality those numbers meant more than ever. The adaptations were necessary for humans to adapt to the changing climate, but importantly for the party, it helped create a loophole that took away the working-class vote. If you were 50% technology you couldn't vote.

The President pointed at Roger. "Are you lying, Roger? I'll use the scan thing."

"The scan thing?"

The President nodded. He meant the Cephalochromoscope. It could read and take near video quality of GA+ Sims, something he required for all his staff after many of the staff in his first White House betrayed him. Roger needed to change the subject.

"Sir, your numbers are excellent with the base, there is no reason to worry about chatter with the 50 P population."

"Assholes," Hewitt moved his hand like a mouth. "Cyborg yap-yap, don't mean shit." Hewitt looked at the old men who were secretly kept alive by technology. "No offense."

"Losers, in Canada." The President said directly to Roger. He expected him to understand and he thought he did.

"Oh yes," Roger spoke slowly, unsure he was on the right track. "The farmers?"

"The farmers. We have worker riots. It is their fault, not mine." The President waved his hand. "In the cities over distribution, mass shootings at an all-time high, a goddamn embarrassment, all liberal cities. Right, they are liberal cities."

The truth is there were no liberal cities, but it was not a good time to make that point. As the global temperature rose, the only crops to be grown consistently were Taro and Amaranth, and only in northern Russia and Canada. Thus, Foodle was invented combining both into a nutritional mush, which the public accepted as long as their minds could translate it in the Sim to be whatever flavor and meals they could simulate. The riots in the cities were not well-known; the younger workers who grew up on Foodle loved it, but...

"I think the President is on to something. We blame this on the Lib-tards," Hewitt smiled. "There must be some way this is their fault."

They employed a few political operatives to play the role of liberals for this very reason. The consequence of the Second Revolution and ridding Great America of liberals is that they had to invent someone to serve their role.

"Woke farmers?" The President pointed at Hewitt, "Regulations out of control."

"They allow unions in Canada right?" Hewitt was proud of himself for thinking of this angle.

Roger sighed. This was all like a broken record. He had had these meetings before. "Mister President, we need to make sure Canada keeps up Foodle production for at least the next year."

The President nodded. He understood the date. The upgrades to the Sims were coming online. Hewitt looked confused.

Roger looked at the grandson. It ran in the family. "You read any of the briefs, seen any of the ads for Heaven for the Living?"

Hewitt was uncomfortable, he squirmed in his chair. "Heaveneers. Those wackos that think they will live forever."

"It is our business dipshit," The President shook his head. "A forever Sim, with family plans and reasonable rates, no longer maintained by hand. A great deal."

He is conveniently leaving out many of the tough sells of the heaven program, but they were all facing some hard realities about life here in America. The President leaned back behind his desk, looking at Roger.

"Greenstone here, he and his whole family have a down payment on their slice of Heaven."

Roger didn't like where this was going.

"You're not logging back in till Canada starts shipping raw Taro, Foodle shipments, the whole deal. You too Little Huey." The President looked at Roger. "He doesn't like that name, I call him Little Huey now, I used to just call him Huey."

Sometimes he wanted praise for his nicknames, Roger didn't need Little Huey explained but he knew the man was proud of himself. Roger just stood up. "If you'll excuse me, I have work to do."

3

THANKS TO A TIP from the Runcible family, Kai's day was off to a better start than yesterday, she was able to pay off the Dream Circuit, as well as her bed and bathroom control. Shutting off ads and helped her relax a little. The gameplay was solid and she made progress to get up to the 300 level. Community play was getting crowded and she thought about looking into another game. As she waited for the elevator to the Skyport, she was surprised not to see George. He was like clockwork. She looked back to the door of his apartment, a few doors from hers.

A door two down from hers opened and her neighbor Erika stepped out and used her palm print to lock her door. She was leaving for her job at Foodle Distribution. She kept her dreadlocks tied back and wore rose makeup that helped her dark skin glow. They always smiled at each other but rarely spoke. Kai was impressed by her outfit, it looked beautiful, far too elaborate for hauling Foodle.

"I love that skirt," Kai smiled as they waited for the elevator.

"Thanks for re-posting me yesterday," Erika smiled at her.

Kai smiled but had no idea what she was talking about. She didn't even follow Erika; didn't see her posts and she certainly didn't repost her.

"It's a new firm and everything is social engagement. So, it really helps, thanks."

Kai nodded as if she knew what she was talking about. The elevator dinged just before it opened. Only one other resident leaned against the back corner, he was holding a scooter helmet and came from the basement, his brow sweat-soaked, having worked some night shift. Erika said hello and while she looked at him, she opened her Manager and her all social hubs, she typed Eri—, a post came up. *Erika Shaw-Thomas new GA+ membership councilor for Southeast Los Angeles (YOU re-posted).* That didn't make any sense. Kai didn't remember reading this post, let alone reposting it.

Erika stepped into the elevator and wrapped a scarf around her head. Kai almost let the doors close on her as she failed to remember reposting Erika. The doors hit Kai and reopened as she dropped her Manager slide into her pocket. Erika covered her face and Kai felt stupid. She didn't follow Ericka, and no memory of friending her on any platform. She would've been jealous of a new gig post, so she would have remembered that.

The door closed and they rose quickly. She forgot about the post when she realized that Ericka had covered herself completely.

"Shit, should I have checked the weather?" Kai bit her bottom lip.

"You have Gogs in your bag?" Erika asked.

Kai reached into her work toolkit and pulled out her red-tinted smart goggles that were connected to her Manager. Erika had green-tinted goggles but held them in her hand as they rose. The elevator stopped on fifty-two, and the other guy got out, leaving them alone for the last eight floors.

"Thanks for the follow, it means a lot to connect with my neighbor," Erika said as she tightened her scarf.

"Of course," Kai nodded, it wouldn't serve any good to tell her she didn't remember following her. She put on her Gogs as the elevator slowed. The right lens synced up with the Ganglion implanted in her eye, she used it to select the Manager interface. The door opened with a woosh, and the push of the Santa Ana winds almost knocked her off her feet. Her eyes were protected but she had to keep her mouth closed as grit blasted out of the high desert into her face. She forgot about it quickly. She had a waiting call from the office.

There was no point in picking up the call in the dust-off. The tram sounded its horn, since you couldn't see or hear it coming, they would only open the doors for twenty seconds on a day like today. She rushed with the small group trying to get on. She was the only one dumb enough to not have a scarf and spit out sand as she activated the call on her Manager.

"Kai here."

"Kai, Darling what took you so long," Her boss Darlene claimed to be a fifty-year-old woman who worked out of their Studio City branch. No one had met her, and some of the Janies thought she was actually a dude working from GA+. Her voice echoed in her ear implant; her image was projected on the lens of her right Goggle. A round-faced woman with her hair in a cute bob, she could be an avatar.

"My shift doesn't start for an hour."

"Change of plans, you have been referred to a new client directly by the GA+ AI server itself."

"Wait, what? I have a 9:30 with the Andertons in the Santa Monica towers, they're waking today for a stretch out and a walk..."

"I have already assigned Cuba to the case; he lives closer anyway."

"Cuba? He is clumsy and lazy; he barely cleans. The Andertons are very particular."

"Cuba is on his way. Go to Union Station and catch a Metrolink to Santa Ana."

"Surface? Darlene, it is spitting desert out there, I am not dressed for the oven either." She saw the annoyance on Darlene's face in the right glass of her goggles.

"Go home if you have to, you don't have to be there till noon, but take a sidearm, NRA says anything south of the 10 is under Lone Wolf warning until winter cool down."

Kai would have to get off at the next stop and wait for the reverse tram. She didn't want to.

"Why can't I just keep my schedule?"

"Darling, please this is not a randomly generated request. The master program selected you for Mister Mayerson, who is the son-in-law of Roger Greenstone, the President Supreme's chief of staff, they are paying three times your standard hourly rate."

"Six times, probably, three is what you are telling me."

"I am going to ignore that hurtful comment."

"I don't give a flurk about him or his president."

"You can act cool all you want but you need Kibble and coin like the rest of us."

"Fine," Kai pulled the cord to activate the next stop. "I'm turning around."

"Nobody wants to bake dirtside when they can be digital sweetheart if there is one truth, we gotta accept before the next century...."

"Darlene, I don't need a lecture."

"Oh, sure thing honey, but guess what you are going to get one. As I was saying, the mind is a terrible thing to waste."

"That's it? The mind?"

"Yes, terrible, terrible thing to waste."

Kai shook her head. "It's all terrible things to waste, all of it, pretty ironic for your generation to lecture us."

She reached up to the kill switch on her goggle strap and ended the call as the tram slowed to a Skyport. She looked around to wave goodbye to her neighbor Erika, she was zoned, either in a Sim or tripping on street sauce. Either way, she was in no state for a goodbye. The doors opened and Kai closed her mouth before entering the dust-off.

***

The Foodle Center suffered under an early morning rush. The temperatures climbed and Texas law required businesses to close when the surface level got above one-twenty. Upper Austin would carry on almost as normal, but if you couldn't exist uptown you had to get shopping done at nine AM or the stores would close. The shopping carts were filled with Foodle powder packets, hydration tabs, and cooling shirts. Tempers flared. Anxious parents who couldn't leave their children at home were spraying them with misters, more than one had passed out lying down in the shopping carts next to the supplies. The registers were working as quickly as they could.

Folks who prepaid tried to sneak out of the store, but desperate people waiting saw them. More than one fight broke out. Why wait to pay? You could grab the cart of prepaid stuff and try to make it to your Auto. Many tried.

Pat Conley watched from his air-conditioned Auto for more than an hour. He spent most of his time logged into GA+, he was just two years of work from earning enough for himself, and five years from getting his whole family a gold plan. He had been dragging at work, only to discover their family Janie was cutting their Foodle, by stealing half and watering down the mix they used. His mind slowed as his earthly body wasted away. Now he saw why.

There just wasn't enough Foodle to go around and these parasites that couldn't afford to have the basics so they took it out on all the hard-working individuals who could. He had thought about this a lot. He knew what would happen now, he watched the NRA forecasts carefully 93% chance of a mass shooter at the Foodle port. He knew exactly what he was, a good guy with a gun, protecting the Foodle that was promised to hard-working families.

He was ready when he saw the man in the tactical gear get out of the car, and swing his AR-15 forward ready to go directly into the crowd.

"Let's fucking go!" Pat yelled in his car and pulled out his Glock. Finally, he was the hero he always dreamed of being.

Two hours later Kai turned off the sync to her Aver and gameplay as the Tram started to dip toward ground level and Union Station. The dust storms had calmed down a bit and she could see the shape of the LA river canal had been covered in concrete and a cooling system to keep what water remained from evaporating in the heat.

The tram landed on the tracks next to the commuter trains and pushed through the exterior bubble that protected loading and unloading, the electric shield was meant to keep out the surface-level heat. The natural humans that stepped off the tram dripped sweat immediately. Kai could smell them with her augmented nose. She kept the outer tints on her goggles engaged, and the inner lens glowed with reports, the temp in the building, the next track where her train left from, and an NRA mass shooter forecast.

Her Manager connected to the station's network and bought her seat for the Metrolink. She received a text message from the White House switchboard requesting a conversation with Chief Greenstone. She agreed to the time, which was two minutes after her train left.

She stepped into the tunnel that connected all the tracks and froze when a shooter alert popped across her left lens. Three active shooters in the current zip code. This happened when you traveled so low in the hotbox. She didn't pay for the up-to-the-minute tracker so she only knew that the gunmen were in the current postal zip code.

Searching the station's database, she found one shooter that was on the west side of the station near the ride-share pick-up. She relaxed a bit, it was a large complex, and it was likely that a citizen would handle the situation long before she was at risk. There was a family pushing suitcases onto the loading dock for the same train and they were not in a panic. Several people on E-scooters flew through the station, barely looking where they were going.

"Morning," She smiled at the mother who was too stressed from herding three children to acknowledge her. A beautiful piano rendition of a song by 20th-century artist David Bowie echoed in the tunnel. The piano was being played by a remote artist, the elegance contrasted with a hooded Sauce dealer, who held baggies with pills and wetware drops of 6-00-6 known in the hotbox as sauce. The origins of 6-00-6 were for regulating body temp in heatwaves, natural humans barely feel it, but augments and cyborgs are treated to a brief but powerful euphoria and less pain when interfacing with mechanical and biological joint intermixing. It helps with the wetware interface, but for techies, it was highly addictive, she had a friend who kept $100 jars of Sause in his fridge, he had nothing but Foodle smoothies and 6-00-6. His place was known to teenage techies as the Sauce Shack.

Kai walked to the train that waited on the track, as it started its route here in the city. She sat down in her seat and the Manager buzzed at the incoming call. Kai looked up at the security camera and waved.

"Kai Dame? This is the White House switchboard I have Chief Greenstone ready for you."

"Yeah, that's me but you know that. I suppose I can chat."

She set the slide up to film her from the back of the seat in front of her. She pushed her Goggles up like a headband pushing her short multi-colored hair back. She smiled, no reason not to. She wasn't a fan of his boss, but he was paying her well.

"Hello there," She tried to sound like someone you would trust with the bodily functions of your father-in-law.

"Miss Dame, Can I..."

"Just Kai, Miss Dame was my grandma."

"I suppose you know who I am."

"My crew chief Darlene filled me in. She was very impressed."

"I have an important position to offer."

Kai nodded, he thinks highly of himself, noted. "How can I help you Chief? Should I call you Chief?"

"Mister Greenstone, please. Kai, my father-in-law is not your typical client, he is a traditionalist, He taught philosophy at Cal State Fullerton, and some might say he is a Luddite. prefers to not log in to GA+ at all."

"If don't might me asking, what am I needed for? I don't do natural elder care."

"I don't want to overstate his aversions; he does log in to spend time with his daughter and our kids. My wife and her father were very close when she was young."

"Ahh, well that sounds a bit more reasonable."

"His care is a priority; I am close to retirement, and we are soon getting gold-level membership."

She understood. They were going to be Heaveneers, the next level of simulation, but one with no return. One shot, and they needed to convince

Papa Mayerson to log in with them or it wouldn't happen. "Shaking off this mortal coil."

"In a sense," Roger Greenstone sighed. "One of his greatest accomplishments as President. For centuries the religions of the world promised Heaven but Mister President delivered."

"If you can afford it."

"Is there an unreasonable price for eternal bliss?"

Kai ignored the question. "I'll have him ready."

"That might not be so easy," Greenstone didn't share her confidence. "I am dealing with something as soon as I can will be there."

"Here in California?"

"Yes, in the meantime your salary and Foodle rations are tripled and we have given you a guest room in my father-in-law's Conapt. It is a comfortable tower."

"Stay? With Mister Mayerson?"

"Just until I get there."

Kai looked at her Manager as the call ended. She had notifications from her video-port and Friend-Feed accounts, more than thirty of them.

She opened the app and scrolled the notifications. A video she posted last night was off the charts with likes, engagements, and replies. She clicked on the video. It was a meme of another gamer's avatar *Stealth_Gunner22* shooting himself in the foot. It was funny but she didn't remember posting it. She might have been tired but it was not a repost, it looked like something she would have made to antagonize her longtime *Night Warrior* rival.

She opened her settings and looked to see if she had given a social media pass to her aver. Sure enough, the sync was loaded. She didn't like her avatar-making posts, even if they got some engagement. A few of the replies reposted with Kibble tips. She wasn't going to turn down the money but it felt weird. She looked at the replies, her avatar had an almost flirty back-and-forth with a user she didn't know.

She undid the sync setting and turned off the Avatar altogether, she had forty-five minutes before Santa Ana, and she would play herself.

Roger Greenstone hit call ended on his Manager and turned to look back at the camera drone floating in his office. Most of the White House staff were working remotely from GA+. They watched him through the Juvenile class drones, and he could monitor their work through a live cephalochromoscope. They were crunching cam footage from a mass shooter in Austin Texas. Only Hewitt and Greenstone working in the office.

Roger tried to get Hewitt's attention. "There was a shooting in Texas is at a Foodle distribution center, and that is a problem, we need to craft a narrative."

Hewitt was distractedly looking at his Manager, he didn't give a shit except the President wouldn't let him log on until they solved their Taro and Amaranth farmer issues.

"Hewitt?"

"Doctor," He was annoyed to be called upon. He tipped his Manager so Roger could see the video game he was playing and waved him off.

"What about the shooting in Louisville?"

A voice in his implant that he recognized as Kayleigh Miller from their communication and social engagement team spoke up. "That is troubling it was a family of Heaveneers, two months from Gold level going through brain-boxing orientation."

A round of regretful moans have through his ear implant. It was a tragedy really, but one that was difficult to spin without inspiring fear that Gold plus members were not safe from gunmen.

"Were they NRA members?" Hewitt asked but his eyes stayed on the game.

"Hardly think that matters," said Kayleigh.

"Of course, you don't," Hewitt circled his ear with his finger knowing only Roger saw him.

"We have our good guy in Texas," Roger tapped his pen on his desk. "What do we know about the gunman in Louisville? Was he a liberal?"

"He was now," Hewitt laughed. No one else was amused. "Is he 50-P?"

"Sixty-one percent human," replied Kayleigh.

"A full person legally, what a shame," Hewitt looked at Roger who took the jab with a sigh. After the Second Revolution, it was Roger who insisted they needed enough liberals to evoke as the bogeyman. The longer the left wing had been gone, the more the techies became the bogeyman. The hypocrisy of demonizing technologically augmented was not lost on Roger, but the lack of self-awareness around him was something the younger Hewitt found hilarious.

"We control the narrative." Roger knew what to say he had long ago given up feeling bad about any of it. He knew they were wrong; he was just past giving a shit. Things with the climate were bad, it was hard to admit the libs and the tree huggers were right but it pushed innovation. They were building a better life for those who had earned it. If they had to massage the facts here and there it was something he would live with.

"Okay, Huey, Mister smarty pants, how you spinning this?"

"Roger, I thought you'd never ask, Thanks to our thirty-nine percent red-blooded great American Patrick Conley of Austin Texas we have the blueprint to save our country. The libs have tried to make it impossible to defend ourselves, what we need is a security force, boots on the ground of certified good guys with a gun."

Roger nodded and pointed at the younger man. "Sounds like the Doctor is in the house."

Hewitt winked. "Boom."

"Leaves me to deal with Canada."

Hewitt gave him a finger gun before leaving.

4

Mayerson's apartment was in the tallest residential tower in Santa Ana, it was only a few blocks from the train station. Kai wrapped herself in cooling scarves and walked. She was a little jealous of the Janies getting in the elevator for the Skytram. She wasn't the only Janie working at the tower but the others probably lived more locally and traveled up in the thinner, cooler air. She passed a boarded-up Foodle store, and a neon OPEN sign flashed telling Kai that it was fortified for the dust storms, she knew from reading Mayerson's file, that the overnight staff considered the old man a regular. His Janies offered to bring his shipments, but he came down a few nights a week and bent the ear of the staff. He knew all their names and considered them friends.

The building had a security gate that connected to her Manager and opened automatically. "Mister Mayerson lives on level sixty-five apartment 12. Welcome to Santa Ana Towers please enjoy your stay." The building spoke with a soft robotic voice. The air in the lower level was still thick and warm, she didn't unfold her cooling gear until she was standing in the elevator.

The carriage climbed on the north side of the building and provided a view of the sprawl spreading north toward the city. She reached out to hold on as they rose, but her view was obstructed by a video ad for Gold Level Heaven. The video looked like a montage of early 21st-century life, the voice was President Supreme himself.

39

Heaven is the America of your choosing. Where men are men, women are women. Hunt for your own food, and value God—you can and will live as God and country intended with a gold-level Sim membership... <Skip Ad>

Kai skipped it and got a clear view of the sprawl. Towers upon towers rose to the sky and blocked the view of the city. A tram floated by as it climbed to the sky an ad for Pegasus Janie Services of Orange County played targeting her. It was a surprise at this distance and so fleeting, but it must have sensed her optics because it was designed for worker recruitment. The massive screen on the tram read "*Work for a union shop and earn twice the coin.*" The ad sent her a link and offered an instant ten-coin tip if she clicked.

The targeted ad had no idea how much she was making today, she let the tram fly on without clicking. The sixty-fifth floor felt comfortable as she stepped off. She heard the amplified sound of an argument. It took her a moment to realize it was the sound of a television. This was a senior tower after all, who else still watched flat 2D Television? When you visited the towers of the wealthy the doors opened for free, no coins disappeared from your account when you rode the elevators.

She knocked on apartment twelve. Nick Mayerson opened the door and let out some cool air. He wore a faded Cal T-shirt and long pants. His grey hair was carefully combed, and he put effort into his appearance, just as his apartment looked tidy but lived in.

He had an ancient laptop computer set up on his dining room table and shelves loaded with books. Kai scanned the titles; she had never seen so many outside of a library or a museum. His balcony looked out across to the ocean on the other side of Huntington Beach and Costa Mesa. She walked up to the glass and got a good look at the greenish-brown water of the coastline. She was stunned.

"Yeah, the ocean."

"It's beautiful."

Mayerson waved her in. "You have no idea; I remember when the water was the same blue as..." He pointed at her eyes. Kai blushed a little and put her bag on the floor. His stare lingered a moment, older folks did that. They always thought they could see the technology, she had a tiny bit of makeup with a little glitter, which made it harder to detect the augments to her skin. It was strange to be greeted by a person. She could see his pod, it looked unused practically new.

"The coastline is dead, the heat drome killed off all the ocean life that couldn't migrate deeper or adapt, the water used to be refreshing for a swim, it is just awful now. So, you are my new Janitor?"

"Call me Kai," she shook his hand. He offered her a seat. She thought about telling him that word was offensive to most in her field.

"I can take care of myself," his voice was thick with anger.

"I introduced myself."

He nodded "That was rude, Nick Mayerson, you can call me Nick. I don't need a Janie."

"Your family feels differently." Kai glanced over at his books, and he smiled with a bit of pride.

"I'm a retired professor. Philosophy mostly, but some ethics."

"Cal State Fullerton?"

"Teaching yes, I'm a UC Berkeley grad, before the second rev."

She pulled up options for humorous banter, and selected sarcastic option #2 "So you're a radical?"

He laughed, a signal that she chose wisely. "Hardly, when such a thing existed, imagine my horror when my beloved Miranda marries the President's chief of staff. Well, he was just a congressman at that point."

She looked at her menu for options. The look on his face told her he could see her scanning options.

"Am I talking to a person or a computer?"

His question offended her, but she understood what he was asking. "You don't use Convaid?"

"Besides the one I was born with?"

It made her nervous to have conversations without it. It was easy to say the wrong thing. To offend people, or create drama. She flipped off her suggested text. It felt a little like stepping off a cliff. "Sorry, it's just me I swear."

Nick Mayerson laughed. "Don't be nervous, just be yourself."

He was amused at how nervous she suddenly was. She sat up straight, trying not to give him the satisfaction. She lied. "I only use Convaid for work. Company policy."

"Bullshit," Nick laughed. "You know I have trained the programming I was born with my whole life. Didn't even try. I conversate *au naturale*."

"If I use it, I'm still being myself, it just helps."

"What does that mean? Who are you, Kai?"

She understood where this was heading and she didn't like it. He was questioning her humanity. She got a feeling the more she challenged him the better.

"Are you asking as a client? Or as a philosopher?"

Nick Mayerson smiled. "I believe the answer is yes to both. You are, after all, here to care for me, and the ethics of existence are the questions I spent a career pondering."

"If your implication is that I am less human than you, I find the suggestion offensive."

"Many find the very nature of 50-P...uh people to be offensive."

"They are assholes."

He laughed at that. He pointed at the bookshelf. "Kant."

"Can't what?"

With some effort and a groan, he pushed his old bones out of his chair and pulled a book off the shelf. "Not can't, but Kant. Spelled K-A-N-T. He was a Prussian philosopher."

She activated a search, "Immanuel Kant."

"You want to prove to me that you are human? Doing net searches on your internal server is not the way."

Kai hated having this type of relationship with a client, but he seemed to enjoy the back and forth. She looked over at the pod, He dropped the book about Kant on her lap.

"I don't want lectures from someone who lives part-time in a Sim. Many of us are working our asses off trying to afford what you take for granted."

"I only Sim to see my grandkids, my daughter…"

"Is it really them?"

Nick laughed and pointed at her. "That is a fair question. If I wanted, my daughter Miranda could appear ten years old to me forever. I could request that."

"Why would you do that?"

"I wouldn't, but when Miranda was ten she loved me the most. It was a special time before all this technology and the heat. She chooses her appearance."

"That is why we work so hard to get to GA+."

He turned back from his bookshelf and smiled at her. "Fools. Not you, my dear. It is a world for fools."

"That sir, if you don't mind me saying is the sound of privilege. Look around, you don't have to pay to use your bed, your bathroom, or your kitchen. Your Conapt is a part of your membership, and that machine…well you have…you have no idea how much people would sacrifice to have one."

"Bertrand Russell believed that machines ended a period of misery that the human race entered with the advent of agriculture. He was underestimating the power of machines to weaponize misery. Ask chickens or pigs that end up on assembly lines. No wait. Don't… I ask you, Kai."

"Ask me what?"

"Do you think it fair that your generation has suffered when you've never been in the ocean, exposed your natural skin to the air, or gone shopping without checking for the Lone Wolf forecast? Do you think it fair that your bullies have access to you twenty-four hours a day, even more hours than *actually* exist in a day if you run Avers on multiple streams?"

Kai walked over to his pod. Years she spent cleaning and maintaining their operation for people who could afford it. Never sure if she ever would. Here, this Great American life sat unused and she was being lectured about what was fair from a man who didn't value it.

"Your family wants to see you."

"Shut up and plug in, Mister Mayerson.' That is what you are thinking."

She dropped the book he handed her by the Janie tool kit she carried. "You can do what you want, but I am going to move into the guest room. Your father-in-law has paid for the whole week."

"I'll love the company," Nick Mayerson walked slowly toward Kai. "You didn't ask me why I suggested the book."

He leaned on the pod, so close to her she could smell the coffee on his breath. "Kant believed knowledge lived up here." He pointed at his head. "Independent of experience. What would he think of this life in the machine?"

Kai didn't know what to say. He was making her uncomfortable.

"I need to unpack but you should see your family," she said.

He mock-saluted her. "We eat real food in this home," he said. "Before any travels, mental or otherwise."

Her body was not used to real food, and frankly, she thought eating was disgusting. It was something that she told herself she had to get used to. This man hated GA+, but he was her ticket there. She had to keep him happy and figure out a way to convince him that he needed to join his family.

"I'll be back in twenty minutes, Mister Mayerson. Your family wants to see you."

5

A BEAD OF WATER came down the stalk of the flower onto her finger, it startled her. The water was cold and that little drop was enough to cause a shiver. The flower was purple with swirling white mixed into the surface, and was more vibrant than she had ever imagined. "Beautiful," she said.

"Lean down. Get it right on your nose."

She was confused. He laughed at her.

"They look beautiful, but the smell..."

She leaned down close to the flower. It tickled her nose.

"Closer. It won't hurt you or your nose."

She got closer and smelled it. Faint, like an echo at first. She had smelled many things in her life but this was sharp, powerful, and gave her a certain kind of ecstasy she had never felt. It ran through her, overpowering her every sense. She coughed, shook, and got light-headed. This made him laugh.

The Museum of Human Experience appeared to be the size of a shopping mall, expanding around them with a campus of interactive experiences meant to highlight the sensations that could be easily forgotten. They had a whole world to choose from, but Nick Mayerson wanted them to be here. He admitted that it bored his grandchildren, who were raised in GA+, but he also knew the effect the tour would have on Kai. Those who lived in the Sim have a lifetime of experiences meant to trick their brains into believing. Kai is the one who never had a life like this, and he enjoyed watching her have these experiences.

Nick's daughter was late. Time in the Sim world was synched to DC at all times. As a matter of economic policy, the Sim didn't need Twenty-Four hour days, per se, but Kai understood the human mind needed the familiar rhythms. The thing she always had to factor in was the lack of heat. She wasn't cold, but the lack of heat was the thing that centered her in this simulated world.

"This is a lot to take in, I know." Kai knew he was pleased with himself. The museum was curated mostly for the benefit of younger Simmies, who had spent only a tiny minority of their existence IRL.

"You didn't have to come here," she said. "I didn't even have to log in."

"My daughter wants to meet you I think."

Kai had chosen a professional Aver. She was wearing her Janie uniform, and sporting a straighter blond version of her short hair. Nick Mayerson was Simmed in an Aver that looked as old and disheveled as the man she hooked into the pod. Her guest membership connection was not as strong as his, so she couldn't imagine what all these experiences would feel like in full force. She twisted her index finger to pull up the directory.

Taste →

She wasn't sure she could handle that room. She felt Nick looking at her.

"You're afraid?"

"Where is your daughter?"

Nick gave her a skeptical look. "My mother only lived in the 20th century. She died in 1998, he said. "She didn't even live as long as my daughter. I often think about what she would think of this brave new world."

He was changing the subject too. Without the benefit of Convaid she hesitated to respond. That never stopped the retired professor.

"Her home was her castle. She grew up in a time and place so different from our world. it was more than technology," he said. "She kept her home tidy."

"Her IRL space?" As soon as she asked the question, she felt stupid. That was the only space she had back then. Most people didn't care what their IRL looked like. It was a part of being a Janie that she never understood. Those Simmies who wanted a nice spot for their pods. Who gave a shit?

"She was a smart woman, and…"

"Dad!"

Miranda Greenstone saved them from a lecture. She was alone, with no children. No famous important husband. Her avatar was subtle, a flowing dress, a summer hat and a pair of sunglasses hung in the center of the dress to pull down her cleavage an extra inch. She was beautiful, but Kai hadn't grown accustomed yet to the natural beauty in the Sim. She turned and offered a hand.

"You must be Dad's new…uh."

"Janie is fine. I am not offended."

"One never knows these days some people want titles like…"

"I'm just Kai. Call me Kai." She smiled, and knew Nick enjoyed the awkward exchange. "I'm not here, just, please…"

"Nonsense, my father values connection as you can see by his choice of venue."

Nick Mayerson hugged her. She held him for a moment, lingering in the hug. It was a curious thing for Kai to watch. She had been born just before the Sim revolution, and her family had been support class for as long as she could remember. Her parents were rarely home when she was growing up, and when they were, they were often too tired to show affection. During the massive heat waves, before the buildings were designed to rise over the heat domes, the temperatures were stifling. She didn't have one memory of a hug like that in her life. It wasn't something she ever missed or thought about before.

"Let's get lunch and talk." Miranda took off her hat and her hair was unnaturally perfect underneath. Of course, it was. Kai realized that, for a moment, she had forgotten she was in a Sim. Kai nodded but didn't know if they would just appear in the restaurant or if they had to travel there. Nick picked up on her confusion.

"There is a café here at the museum," he said. "Quite good, but it is easier to program good food than actually cook it."

"Dad, can't we just enjoy lunch?" She hooked his arm and walked with him. Kai lost track of them as they walked through the Taste wing of the Museum. Miranda told Nick about the grandkids, their new jobs, and the careers they were building. Kai didn't listen. She snuck a look at the stats for gameplay and wished she was logged in to the game instead of at this Sim museum. Each display they passed represented a different culture from the world and the cuisine that matched it. The smells carried teasers of various flavors to her nose. Her net identified them as freshly baked bread from Lebanon, soft noodles from Southeast Asia, and cooked meats from Mexico.

It made her dizzy. Her menu floated in her vision and gave her the option to order any of these items. Nick held up a finger to pause his daughter's report on the family. "Try the Ramen. It is mostly soup. You don't want to eat anything too heavy the first time."

"Live it up, my dear," Miranda said. Your appetite is as big as your eyes in GA+."

They sat at the table and the prompt to order hung over the table.

"Do you trust me?" Miranda smiled. "Dad, she should experience your favorite."

She tapped the menu, and a wait-bot rolled over to the table. "Welcome to Café at the Museum of Human Experience. Our menu features data on more than one billion uploaded menus from restaurants preserved in the cuisine and establishment database."

"We would like to order from Gio's Chicago-style pizza in Wrigleyville, North Clark Avenue."

The lights on the wait-bot seemed to flash. "Accessing, what year would you like?"

Nick took a deep breath as if savoring the idea of it. "Maybe the 80s, say 1985?"

"Excellent choice, Gio's was the Sun-Times deep dish pick for the third consecutive year. I have informed the kitchen." A screen floated in the air over the table. EXPRESS or REALISTIC WAIT TIME. Miranda went for realism and poked the menu. The wait-bot rolled away.

"Enough about us Dad…"

"Me? Nothing to tell. Reading, cooking, enjoying the view."

"Cooking?"

"When I can get the real stuff. It wouldn't fool my mother, but it seems like food enough for me most days."

"How does his place look? Tell me honestly." Miranda said to Kai. It took her a moment to realize she was being addressed.

"Uh, lived in. Most clients I support live as much time in GA+ as possible."

"Yeah, my father the Luddite. You see Dad, you are the weird one."

"This is all bullshit," Nick waved his hand around.

"And yet," Miranda looked at Kai. "Watch him eat that pizza."

"I'm here," he said. "I come to see you."

"Dad, this world is just as real as yours, if not more real."

"We have separate worlds now?"

"I embrace this world, and I will embrace the next."

Kai could only watch Nick and Miranda go back and forth.

"This again, is a program of engineered sensations, memories of feelings taught to a computer by people," Nick said.

"Sensations are just sensations. How many of your philosophers believed that existence happened in the mind, not with crude things like a body? This is how our minds were meant to live. To be free. This is freedom for the mind. The president made good on his promise to the nation, to make us great and free."

"Can you hear yourself? What of our guest?"

Kai felt like a spotlight turned on her. Miranda smiled at her. "What of her? She is very welcome here."

"As your guest, but she and her fellow Janies…"

Kai waved this off. "Please, I don't want to get involved."

"She is well paid; people need these jobs," Miranda said.

Nick rolled his eyes. "I know exactly where this is going. If you want to go, do it."

"I won't live forever without you."

"You won't live forever, sweet pea. That is not my idea of living."

It went on like that for twenty minutes. Kai was aware of the time because she had never spent this much time logged in as a guest to GA+. They were so involved in the debate over his future that they didn't notice her distraction. She opened a private window and watched her Aver playing patrol.

The wait-bot rolled to the table with the pizza. She smelled it first before it crossed the room, pulling a trail of steam. It was the shape of a wheel, yellow and topped with pieces of food she didn't recognize. Nick had dismissed the simulation almost the entire time they had been logged in, but now that the pizza was here, he savored it, engrossed and acting like any other Simmy.

"Each serving of pizza is called a slice." He lifted a wedge of it and it seemed hard to hold together. He gave the first slice to his daughter who held out a plate. Nick pointed at hers and Kai held the plate out for him. She watched them eat and studied the method. Once she took her first bite it was shocking. The heat, the texture, the flavors. It overwhelmed her. The Sim adjusted as she ate, something she knew natural food didn't do. Raised on Foodle, the experience was heavenly. Warmth, flavor, and texture were all delivered experiences she never had before.

She had a second piece, and as she did she watched Nick loosen up. He and Miranda talked about the beach house they rented during the summers in Laguna Beach. They laughed, smiled and the drama of the last hour was forgotten. She ate the last bite of pizza and felt a curious feeling in her stomach, she had no context to explain it. Nick must have been feeling the same as he rubbed his stomach and leaned back. Miranda enjoyed seeing her father in this state and was relaxed in a way that seemed impossible an hour ago. Kai used their distraction to see what kills and coins her avatar had racked up. The game was always in the back of her mind, no matter what experiences she had inside the Sim.

She missed the end of the conversation. When she looked up, she had to swipe the game monitor out of her vision, and the motion would have given her away if Nick understood the technology.

They stepped out of the front doors of the Museum. The landscape beyond was beautiful, like nothing Kai had seen in reality. The mountains on the landscape had white tops. The buildings barely lifted off the ground, and the air outside felt like it came from a cooling vent. The white puffy clouds didn't bring rain and no one walked around prepared for dust storms. She had never seen so far without being above the heat domes.

"You ready to go home?" Nick smiled at Kai.

She ignored the fact that they never left his home, but she wasn't ready at all. With every fiber of her being, she wanted to stay here, to live in this beauty. But she knew the Sim would start to degrade for her soon, as guest passes were limited. She was coming up on two hours. Paid members never had to leave because they had someone like her to take care of them. She knew she would also have to leave the Sim first as she was a guest on his pod's signal.

Miranda kissed her father on the forehead. "Please Dad. I can't do it without you."

He kissed her hand, and suddenly his smile was gone. Her parting words hit Nick Mayerson like a bomb. She said it just as he prepared to log out.

Kai looked around, the clear sky suddenly looked like the inside of a Foodle tube, brown murky, and clouded. Just like that, she felt the overworked air conditioning holding off the subtle heat of reality. Kai opened her eyes and Nick Mayerson's apartment formed around her. She heard the purring of the GA-pod cooling down. There was a bell sound, the signal that the link to GA+ was severed.

Kai jumped up to open the unit. The older Mayerson smiled at her as she propped him up. He looked a little sad. He took a few deep breaths as she reached to the bottom of the unit and pulled a Foodle bottle from the feed tube, green crust caked the outside.

"Depressing."

"Huh?" Kai wondered.

Nick pointed at the bottle. "That is our pizza, isn't it?"

Kai shrugged and threw the bottle to the recycling bin and bank-shot it off the wall. Kai looked back at the sad, older man. Just a minute ago he was beaming and happy with his daughter. So much had changed in that minute.

"What did she say that upset you? I don't understand."

Nick sighed. "She wants me to join the family in Heaven."

Kai's eyes got wide. "They have the money for gold level? What are you waiting for?"

Nick laughed. "I know the perfect life, but..."

He looked away from her and out the window toward the ocean.

"Nick, you have to. I mean I hear some people don't even remember it is Sim."

"Kai, have you ever wondered if you were already in one? If it was so believable..."

"No one would choose to live like this."

He raised an eyebrow. She knew she stepped in it. He had told her over and over that he chose to live like this. He was fighting with his beloved daughter because he chose to live like this.

"I'm sorry, I turned off my Convaid for you, so you are going to have to handle me saying dumb and insensitive shit.

He shook his head. "Speak your mind, Kai."

"Nick, everyone wants the gold plan. If I had the coin, I mean..."

Nick sniffed the air and fought tears. "The cost is so much more than money. It is called Polyencephalic Fusion..."

"I know what it is called, Nick. But, you'll be together."

"I am not ready to give up my body."

She understood that attachment to the body was difficult for most humans under 50-P. She couldn't understand it. She had been replacing parts of her body one piece at a time for as long as she could remember. She didn't want to push him. She knew part of her job was to convince him, but her instinct was to wait and try harder to understand him first. Like many 50-P, she had no choice. Adapt-to-survive, tech-to-thrive. Surgery was paid for, but you entered the workforce with debt. Still, it was the only way she could escape. She had fought her whole life to have the very thing he was turning down.

"You understand, right?"

She didn't. The pizza and the smell of the flower lingered in her memory. The feeling of cold and clean air. She couldn't understand why anyone would not want that experience forever. She felt anger toward Nick. This great privilege he was offered and he didn't care. She needed to get away from him.

"Can I help you get ready for bed?"

She wanted to game. She wanted to connect to her life, and she was feeling a new pressure to excel in the game.

"Yeah, thanks for understanding."

6

Roger Greenstone braced himself when the Auto came out of the canal to the dry streets in Silver Spring, Maryland. The pavement had been buckling under the heat and battering from storms for months, so the ride was bumpy. The surface temperature was already 97 degrees, and this time of morning the streets were busy with delivery drones and support staff trying to beat the coming midday heat. Most Janies completed their commutes by 8 AM to avoid the heat.

When he sent the RSVP for Stephen's Boxing ceremony, he expected he would have to be logged in from GA+. He had never been to one of these IRL. He jumped at the chance when the calendar notification popped up on his Manager. His family would be right behind him if he could get his father-in-law on board. It was a chance to see what this process would look like.

Stephen Baxterman had worked with the President since his first campaign, one of the first career Republicans to bet on the right candidate. In all those decades, he never stopped mocking the man behind his back, and when Stephen faced indictments and constant legal fees, their relationship was strained. Roger and Stephen had bonded over the years, having never hidden how they felt about the man they worked for. Over the years and many late-night drinks, Stephen admitted they had been wrong about everything except the Gold-level Heaven Sim. Roger was drunk and was glad his friend didn't remember the argument. He felt strongly that they wouldn't need the Sim world if they had not fucked up the real one. But, they had more money than they could count and the gold-level membership, so why feel guilty now?

Like Roger, Stephen saw shaky reports on the simulation tech. The engineers had perfected Polyencephalic Fusion, making communal simulation possible. But the augments to the human brain could not be done inside the skull. The bigger problem was that the detail of the immersion was not entirely convincing until the fifth software update. At this point, Heaveneers were almost entirely fooled. In time, this life would fade into the background as one of those surreal dreams. That is what they had both worked for.

The problem is no one returns from heaven. It was a leap of faith.

You could choose any year, from 1960 or forward to start your Sim. Research showed a year into the simulation and the blend was complete. Anyone suggesting you were living in a simulation would be disregarded as deranged. That was the sales pitch.

"Now arriving at the Silver Spring first Methodist congregation. Would you like the garage or shall I prepare a protective suit?" The Auto asked.

It wasn't even a hundred degrees yet, he knew the Auto was just trying to protect him. The sky was turbulent, the edge of the storm was blowing hot tropical air, but for the moment it was blocking the intensity of the sun enough that he could walk in the front door.

"This is fine." Roger pushed the button that engaged the door and stepped out into the natural air. It was shocking for a moment. It had been years since he felt the surface air. It felt hotter than he was expecting. He walked up the steps and watched the Auto go to park itself.

The Auto from the Heaven-center waited at the backdoor for Stephen and Holly's boxes.

Inside the church, the cool air hit him just in time. The storm had kicked up enough moisture that he wiped his brow as he walked into the sanctuary. The Priest carried a candle and was lighting a row of large candles that lit the stage at the front. Stephen and his wife Holly sat alone in the first pew. Roger saw the cameras next to them. He signed in with his Manager and saw that three hundred and four accounts were logged in to watch the ceremony.

The Janie techs rolled in the stretchers. The surgery would be done in the basement, after the last rites.

Stephen turned around and saw Roger. He walked up the aisle. Stephen was thinner than he had ever been when they worked together. He was rarely off-line in the last decade, a diet of pure Foodle and Sim life had taken this big, imposing man and turned him into a rail-thin shadow of himself.

"What are you doing here, buddy?"

"President has me babysitting his grandson through a dust-up with Foodle farmers up in Canada."

Stephen pointed to a pew, they sat down. "Sounds like a nightmare. Can't say I am jealous."

"You love this shit," Roger looked across the church to the ceremony. "This is more involvement than I expected out of you, Stephen.

"I'm ready," Stephen wiped a little sweat off his forehead. "Holly is the religious one."

"Are you nervous?" Roger asked and he gave away his own nerves.

"Don't be," Stephen laughed a little. "Everyone dies, everyone gets composted in a box, and no one has ever had any real idea what will happen. Not us."

That was the promise of their great leader: an afterlife made possible by technology that left nothing to the chance of the universe. Roger nodded. He had been pitching it his whole career. America in its purest form. We are above the great mystery.

"So, tell me about Canada." Stephen leaned back.

"No, buddy, not on your boxing day; you are retired. No work for you."

"Let me be helpful one last time."

Roger looked at his old friend, knowing it was the last time. Stephen Baxterman was a liberal bogeyman before the Second Revolution. Prosecutors in the last democratic-led DOJ had a hard-on for this man, who they believed would die in prison. He had held the President Supreme's hand through every illegal scheme to stay in office, and eventually, he was right, the liberals would grow tired. They would want to get along, they would want their status and, eventually, they would get down on one knee. He had a way of telling brutal truths that Roger would miss. He never knew anyone as cunning or as brutally pragmatic as Stephen.

"The production has ground to a halt. I need to get up there, but I assume migrant workers in the Canadian fields are not able to work full shifts without augments that put their rights rating past 70-p."

"And they want rights as human beings, at thirty percent human? They are more machine than migrants at this point," Stephen said. "Not a chance. Time to be the world-class asshole you were born to be."

Roger nodded. "The optics are not great, we can't grow Foodle without them, and they feel that gives them leverage."

"Leverage? For the poor bastards depending on Great America Plus, maybe." Stephen laughed. "I've choked down my last Foodle."

The gold-level Heaven Sim was rolling out slowly, but the costs were great and the entry was permanent. Even the President was not ready to log in yet. GA+ maintenance was political, like gas prices had been a hundred years ago. Stephen's good humor about all of this would offend most people, but harsh political realities were part of the language of their friendship. Still, they needed to keep the population fed, with an environment hostile to most crops.

"India is growing food in orbit and the costs are coming down," Roger said. "The Germans and the new Nazi coalition are growing radiation-re-sistant Foodle on Mars. China is working to develop a quicker processing Sim-world, and they could undercut the gold plan."

Stephen waved him off. "Total immersion, they can't come close. They are not close to independent brain function."

"They are saying in the Chinese Sim you can live on other planets. Total fantasy shit. Anything you can dream."

"We need a few more seasons of Foodle before we can roll out enough Gold plans to even process the members pre-sold."

Stephen had the grin he showed off before offering his solution. "Robots, 80-P drones driven by GA+ plus based pilots working the fields. That will bust the unions fast. If they have given that much of their bodies to the technology, they will let drone jocks pilot them for a work day. They aren't crossing the picket line if they are working virtually. Come on Roger this is not rocket science."

Roger nodded. This was not too different from his plan, but he was letting his friend chip in. Holly stood in the aisle as if to ask them what was taking so long.

"I'm glad you are here, Roger."

"Oh yeah?"

"We are boxing in the government data center. We were going to have the Secret Service deliver us."

The center was underground with an independent power system meant to last five hundred years on a single nuclear battery. It was only available for top-level government officials and families.

"Yeah, but where are you going?" Roger tapped his temple.

"We have a farmhouse in Michigan, on a lake, in the fall. I'm planning to forget that Winter is ever supposed to come. The leaves are just beautiful. Holly wrote the program with the Heaven architects, it's perfect."

"Sounds beautiful."

"Will you box us at the data center? Should only take a few hours."

Roger smiled. He hadn't thought about who would do this for him and his family. He could see why Heaveneers would want the ritual of a friend taking part in the process.

Holly walked up the aisle. Stephen stood and held her hand.

"Yeah, let's do it."

⸻

The White House was not pleased with the delay, but Roger had made Stephen a promise. The Auto waited in the Church's air-conditioned garage. The storm had passed over the region and they were in a window of direct sunlight that was warming the region until the next storm, which would hit just before sunset. The whole building was warming up. The air conditioning system was overworked. The church was built in the mid-20th century and the cooling system wasn't designed for today's temperatures.

The surgery was performed by 75-P Techies who were paid to be the hands of surgeons working remotely from GA+. Since patients planned on dying, the operation was made easier. It wasn't something Roger wanted to watch, so he waited in the next room. He heard the drilling and cutting. The body died quickly, and all the tech augments were turned off and removed; their organs already sold and promised to new users.

The only part that could not be damaged was the brain itself. Roger had his Manager out and was typing a series of e-mails that would go out to the leaders of the work crews operating in the northern breadbox. He was about to start enforcing their production schedules and start sending drones to target agitators.

He had sent multiple e-mails when the surgical drone stepped into the room and disposed the bloody smock. The body of the drone didn't need their tech or artificial skin, and its eyes glowed to show it was being controlled remotely. There was a slight lag.

"The operation was a success," a woman's voice said, from the drone body that, through all the tech, appeared to be male.

Two robots came into the room holding metal boxes, with handles so he could carry them. The earthly remains of Holly and Stephen Baxterman were adjusting as they soaked in the Hubrizine that would stimulate the processing centers of their brains long enough for them to be transported to the data center. A single port on the bottom connected them to the server where they could be uploaded into their own personal heaven.

Stephen slid his Manager into his pocket and offered his hand. The boxes weighed about six pounds each, and only half of that was the brains themselves. Roger wasn't used to carrying anything, but he nodded and walked to his Auto.

The air conditioning barely cooled the garage, which was sealed to the outside world. The Auto opened. It had been cooling for several minutes.

Roger could feel the cooling cubes under his skin come to life, so the heat only affected him for a moment. He placed the boxes in the back seat and stepped into the front, behind the wheel, before sliding across to the passenger seat.

"Go for the data center." Roger took his job seriously. He knew as soon as his Father-in-Law was on board, they would be making the trip. This was Nick Mayerson's nightmare. He was attached to his flawed body. Roger felt the glass on the window heat up before the tint adjusted and darkened. The sensors in his inner eye registered the growing radiation levels. The outside temp was thirty degrees north of three digits. None of it was getting better out there in the world. He looked into the back seat at the two brain-boxes and thought a never-ending Fall at a lake in Michigan sounded wonderful right about now.

7

Kai wasn't sure if she was supposed to stay with him. It was strange enough being in someone else's home, but Nick was not like anyone else she knew. He walked around the space cleaning. As a Janie, part of her job was to clean the pods and living spaces for her clients, but very few of her people cared what their homes looked like. She stood there watching him take a damp cloth and clean the surface of his kitchen counters.

"Good night, Kai."

"Should I be helping you?"

He laughed, "I like cleaning."

She nodded and left for the room that was hers. In the doorway, she turned around and saw him scanning the bookshelf. His Manager had access to every book in the world and could read it for him. She knew it was a generational thing, using books, but Nick was born into a world that already had technology everywhere.

"Get some rest, Kai." He knew she was watching him.

He walked over to his chair in the living room and sat down to watch the sun go down over the ocean through the window.. This time of year, it was after nine o'clock when the sun dipped over the horizon. The glass of the window, even this high up, heated under the sun. When he started to read his book, she shut her door and then reopened it with a crack to watch him. She was being paid lots of money to keep her eye on him.

She had ignored her Manager, and the moment she flipped off silence mode it buzzed to life with all the notifications since she left the Sim. She turned off the inner eye menu and looked at her hand-slide. She selected check activity. She wanted to see how many coins her Aver made fighting off gunmen in the game over the last twelve hours.

Bells rang faintly outside her door. At first Kai thought it was a recording that Nick was playing but he stood up from his chair as soon as she heard it. She held up her Manager, sampled the sound, and selected search. Nick opened his balcony door and then she could tell the sound was from outside.

Search results: Orange County Sky Temple at the Santa Ana East tower.

Nick pushed a chair out to his balcony to look at the night sky. Kai pushed the door shut and projected her Manager to the flatscreen monitor that was on the wall.

She expected she see game stats, kill rates per hour, virtual ammunition levels, and the coin she had earned. When she logged on, more than thirty notifications suddenly scrolled on the screen. It was all her activity on the various platforms and social networks. There were comments, likes, dislikes, photos, screenshots, emojis, pokes, and friend requests. More than thirty of them just in the last hour. Kai got a sinking feeling as she scrolled. There were seventy posts she had liked by a Psych-beat band called *Thump* made up of deaf musicians that mentally transmitted beats. She clicked to open a window and felt the beat inside her; the music carried by thought. It was catchy music that made her want to tap a foot, and she thought it was really cool. She felt the urge to like the post, so she moved her thumb and tapped the screen.

The like faded away. She was confused. She felt an instant of panic. I LIKED IT. People will think she hated it. She was afraid her followers would think she hated the hearing impaired. The next notification appeared, then another. Suddenly, the Psych-beat post, and the song was lost in her Manager's long social feed. Every moment it was gone, people would judge her. She knew her followers were composing posts about her Psych beat erasure and disregard for the hearing impaired.

"No, no! Fuck, where is it?"

She searched the Psych Beat page and found the band Thump. They had thirty videos, but she had only heard the one song, so she selected the first one on their playlist. The beat was heavier. It felt like a chorus of bass drummers. The vocalist didn't sing anything resembling English or even words, but she quickly hit the thumbs up. She scrolled and hit every thumbs-up she could and relaxed a little.

What else has her Aver gotten into while she was working? It was supposed to support her, not stress her out. Her thumb kept scrolling, scrolling through likes and meaningless comments like "What up gurl your Aver looks hot as fuck." She bit her lip when she saw multiple dangerous jokes about President Supreme's vain attempts to convince people he was under the legal 50-P threshold.

Nothing her Aver did was out of character. It was all the same reactions she would've had, music and videos she would have liked, but it was a strange feeling seeing an entire online life unfold. Then she saw the notifications timed with her logging into Great America with Nick Mayerson.

The Aver piggybacked her signal and hit the Great America Server, on the data stream that came from the great information center in Oklahoma. Her Aver hit the network and was active, using the connection to access systems throughout the Sim. The notifications felt endless, community groups, message boards, and real estate agents who were throwing pitches at her for virtual homes known as Protophasic Simulation Ports. This level of activity on a guest login was illegal. Much of the coin she earned in the last twenty-four hours was all redirected and no one was going to report a data hobo who was transferring funds. This quickly went from weird to scary.

Everyone chatted with their Aver, mostly in shorthand, and rarely did anyone have to request a chat. It knew she was worried, the Avers were synced, and the Aver knew every damn thing she was feeling. It was hiding.

Hey. A direct text.

Two new notifications popped on the screen. It liked a video posted by her Aunt Susan and posted a request for online ammo trades. Just going on like nothing was happening.

STOP!

The pretty online version of herself faded onto the screen.

"We don't need to talk," Her voice spoke from the speaker on a flat screen on the wall, the camera on her living face watching her from the Manager in her hand. Kai turned down the volume and became a little worried Mayerson would hear them.

"Nick is outside," her Aver said. "Almost everyone from Towers goes out to their balconies when the bells ring, it is set to the temperature…"

"I read the same article," Kai shook her head. "What were you thinking? It is illegal to even scan the GA+ without a membership."

"You'll have one soon. We have to be ready. You focus on the old man and let me handle everything. I'm not doing anything you wouldn't do."

Kai felt stupid and embarrassed. Her Aver of course knew this.

"You always wanted to be this engaged. Your posts are getting more views and likes than ever."

That hurt. Because it wasn't her, at least it didn't feel like it.

"Kai, stop it." Her Aver smiled. "It's you. Really you. I am you. To those people, you are a name and profile picture. Some of your best online friends have been dead for years."

This took her by surprise. She looked at the camera with a skeptical look.

"What are you talking about?"

Her Manager screen flipped under the Aver's control to the profile of Travis_Games_202. The picture in the account was of the man eating virtual sushi with chopsticks that he held in front of his smiling face. They had never met, but they talked about Patrol tactics on-Sim for years.

"He just commented on my music activity five minutes ago."

"Did he? Or did he have a heart attack last year, just thirty coins from a great America upload? He had the pod in his apartment and a contract from New Day Janie to clean Foodle ports monthly when his heart just gave out."

Last year? Kai thought to herself, and the Aver nodded.

"Hey, Avers can tell. Don't feel stupid. It is how he wanted to be remembered."

Kai leaned back on the bed. She accessed a stim and felt the liquid appear under her tongue. She wanted the game. No interest in sleeping. Her Aver represented the part of her that grew tired of the game, but after a day of traveling in the real world, all she wanted to do was play.

"That is more like it. We need the coin, Kai. We are close. So close."

Nick Mayerson felt the natural breeze blow on his face. The air was cooling without the full power of the sun. Even as dusk took hold, he felt it was comfortably hot. That wouldn't stop his neighbors from getting fresh air on their balconies. One of his neighbors, two stories above, played an acoustic guitar. Faintly, a song from the previous century wafted down to him. It was David Bowie or the Beatles, or some other Twentieth-century stuff from before his time. The night was festive on the balconies between the older residents who would cross-talk. Most of them grew up in the earlier stages of the internet.

Leaning over the railing, Nick looked toward the ground and thought about his childhood. His mother used to get so frustrated with him bringing back sand when he came into the house. It covered his shoes and clothes. He spent hours surfing in the summers which seemed to last forever. Now the idea of going into the ocean was nothing more than a quaint memory.

He looked back at the guest bedroom and knew this young woman was sent here, not to babysit him, but to convince him to jump, essentially. Every night he looked over this edge and thought about it. Was it better to die a person or to live as a memory? He would never admit it to Miranda, but he enjoyed being in Great America Plus. He argued against it for so long it was hard for him to admit how much he enjoyed the simple pleasures, especially the ones that the real world couldn't provide anymore.

"Be young again Dad...Surf...Pizza...Chocolate cake."

The thing he missed most was her mother. Lisa died in an accident, nothing could be saved. She never had the chance to grow old. Forty-four years old was the age she was frozen in their memories. Miranda seemed fine having a simulation of her mother. She was convinced that Heaven would trick their minds and they wouldn't know the difference.

Nick understood how she might feel that way. To Miranda, she was mom. Lisa Harris Mayerson was a firm and consistent parent. Miranda would be forgiven if she thought her mother lived only for her. The simulated version of her mother was similar to her memory of Lisa.

The Lisa simulation was a regular dinner guest. A few days earlier, the had met in GA + at Rancho Villa, which had been their favorite beachside Mexican restaurant in Laguna Beach for a sunset dinner. She looked perfect. Too perfect, he thought. In real life, she had a tiny mole on the right side of her neck. It was tiny, but he had kissed it so many times in his life that it bothered him that it wasn't there in GA+. It looked like her. The simulation had learned her voice from old videos, so it sounded like her. It was only when the conversations started that it began to fail.

Lisa had used social media plenty, and the program was trained with her papers, books, and the surviving text messages. The dinners felt like being out to eat with her Facebook and Instagram accounts. This virtual Lisa didn't have the sarcasm that his wife had. Didn't have the puns based on deep-cut German Philosophers. The Sim could talk about Heidegger and the three levels of reality, but she glitched and froze when he made jokes about Binswanging. It was an inside joke they shared only with each other.

It was comforting to be at the table with her, and to enjoy a sunset that looked and felt like a dream. It could almost convince his brain that he was back in this spot with her for real. He offended her the last time, and even as he felt her wrath he felt a little comfort at feeling it. Anger was a part of Lisa's personality, one of the things Miranda rarely saw.

"Are you happy?" Nick asked but realized she was programmed to be content. So, he went deeper. "I mean, are you happy being a program, a series of signals, pre-programmed materials?"

"I don't understand," a little annoyance in her voice.

"I was wondering what Heidegger would have thought of you and this…all this."

"Heidegger was a fucking Nazi."

"You exist. Your creation is different from my Lisa, but you are here."

"Who exactly is your Lisa if not me?"

He exited the program rather than answer. He hadn't reloaded the program since. He had replayed this question a million times in the last week. He had wondered about it himself. Could he be happy without a body? He told himself that at least he would have a soul. That is why they called it Heaven. Your mind survives. Your soul survives.

He stepped inside and shut the door to the balcony. He looked at his bed and then the accursed pod where he went off to Never, Never Land. He was fine walking on ancient, creaking bones and in that moment he felt alive.

8

He wasn't the only person wearing tactical gear on the Skytram. He kept his AR-15 at his side and his Glock never left the holster. Many commuters wore bulletproof vests and it was becoming more common here on the Chicago Sky-Metro to wear commuter-friendly battle helmets. If you had an NRA membership you could detect threat levels and receive automated warnings if the safety on your weapon was switched off. Even now, as Peter scanned the crowd all the armed men and women came up as registered "Good Guys with a Gun."

The sensors couldn't read his intention. Any scanner background checks would find nothing but a good citizen and a God-fearing man. His stop was coming. He had butterflies and thought about just going home as they crossed out of the Upper Downtown loop ring. The stop was at the Ritz Tower on Grand. The data center was across a bridge from the stop. It was the newest building in the city and it reached one hundred and twenty-five floors above Chicago. It was the tallest building in the skyline, but it was the one that had the fewest windows. Inside existed a population larger than some countries here at the end of the 21st century. Peter wouldn't and couldn't bring himself to say he lived in that building. They called it Chicago's Gates of Heaven. When the sun rose over Lake Michigan in the morning, the building looked like a flame from the water.

The government wanted everyone to consider it hallowed ground. For all the people on this train, it was just where they went to work every day. To Peter, it was an abomination. The souls of millions were taken from their bodies, fooled into believing they were in Heaven, when, in truth, their brains were removed and left to function alone. It was an insult to Jesus, who had died for their sins and could never embrace those disembodied souls. The President was a liar who never had Christ in his heart. Never.

The tram pulled into the station, and he was surprised by how many people sat up or moved towards the doors. When he stepped out onto the Skyport outside the Ritz, high above Grand, he was surprised at how hot it was sixty floors above the city floor. He felt the cooling pads come on under his skin. The bright glow triggered his Ganglions. Without them, the bright sunlight would have caused long-term damage to his nervous system long ago. His Manager's menu floated in his vision, and he blinked twice to close a pop-up ad for cool, refreshing Foodle Ice-pops at the Ritz Sky café.

Peter let the Heaven workers walk ahead of him across the sky bridge. He took one look up at the building. It reached to the sky, even from here. He knew he could only free so many souls, but he prayed that Jesus would give him the strength to be his warrior today. The tram doors shut and left for the next Skyport. He couldn't turn around now.

"Help me, Jesus."

He walked the bridge. The sun hung over Lake Michigan. He walked a little faster to check up with the crowd and used his thumb to switch off the safety as he entered the building.

Roger Greenstone was in the air-conditioned boat coming to the dock at the back of the White House when the notification came across his server: *Shooter mass casualties in Chicago.*

He glanced at his Manager briefly and slipped the device back into his pocket. The seal tube airlocked with his boat and kept him protected from the tropical storm swirling chaos above the central Eastern Coast.

John Goodwin, the Secret Service agent who met him, scanned his retina with tech built directly into his eye socket. This agent was born human, but his body had given way to the machine parts long ago. At 70-P he didn't need a pod or require a Janie. His mind was enjoying life in Great America while his body was standing there. Goodwin had worked the president's detail for many years and Roger watched him become more of a machine year by year.

"Morning, Agent Goodwin."

Their technology interfaced inside the scan. It was a strange feeling. Greenstone could see his Manager's menu in the corner of his vision, which Goodwin was scanning for hidden explosives. Goodwin was skilled enough as a Great America Plus user that he could work in the Whitehouse and live a secondary day online. Roger wondered if he was talking to him at all, or if he was a phantom. People who were 70 Percent machines could always give over control to their Aver. They were called ghosts, phantoms, or puppets. Different regions had different slang for it. Phantoms were not all that different but all his auggies and tech were not designed to be hidden like the President's.

When the encephalscan was complete, all his office e-memos came across his Manager, including the request for an emergency meeting.

"Welcome, Mister Greenstone," Goodwin said. "The President is currently logged in and will be meeting you and Secretary Hewitt by link."

As Roger walked, the agent followed him. "Please inform the president I am dealing with an emergency already up in..."

"You have not read about Chicago, have you?" The President's assistant said through her heavy Eastern European accent. She walked through the room right past him, and reminded him of the President's previous wives. The President's staff knew if they didn't hire women he found exotic or sexy, he would lose focus. Yanna was Belarussian, in her twenties. She had been a gift from the longtime dictator of Belarus after President Supreme had him appointed. Thanks to implants, augments, and skin that was anything but natural, she was still as shiny as the gold banisters and towel rack the President had installed in the White House

"I mean, I saw the headlines. Another shooting..." Roger shrugged as he walked into the meeting room. Hewitt was filing his nails, and the President Supreme's Aver loomed over the room on the monitor.

"Read the article asshole," said the leader of the nation.

"Or you could just tell me?" Roger shrugged and put his Manager on the table. He selected the article. This time he pulled up an abstract compiled by the NSA. If they wanted him to address it, he needed the unspun truth.

ABSTRACT: *A gunman with a classic Christian evangelical voting record, and no previous criminal record opened fire in the Chicago Heaven data tower. The damage is extensive. It appears that he detonated a homemade explosive device...*

Roger closed his Manager. He didn't need to read more.

"Very bad, Roger. Very bad."

"We are still gathering information," Yanna forwarded links to everyone. "Twenty-five workers in critical condition. Fifteen dead, confirmed."

"Tell 'em about the Heaveneers, sweetheart," The President said on the screen.

"We can't say exactly yet, but it appears there was damage to several thousand brain boxes that were corrupted, and that led to a cascading failure of the server network..." She didn't finish.

"We're fucked," the President said. "They'll say if we can't be safe in heaven, why get a gold plan? We charge a lot of money for that. Many dollars."

Roger was not surprised that he was already calculating money. He knew decades ago that the President had his unique concerns: his money, his image. Long before he gave way to technological fixes, the man was a vain pile of make-up and hair sculpted to cover how little he had on the top of his head. The first argument he had witnessed as a member of the staff was during the first pandemic. The strap of the face mask was collecting his bronzer make-up. He refused to look "weak" in the mask when his own government was encouraging masks as a lifesaving tool.

"So, we need to work on messaging?" Roger cut to the chase.

"He is not one of ours, I can tell you that. ANTIFA, those Motherfuckers."

"Sir," Roger shook his head and explained this a thousand times. "That particular Bogeyman is a relic of the era before our revolution. This gunman will have a GA+ profile. It will be all about you and Jesus, not ANTIFA."

"Plus, we just did a trick in Texas," Hewitt was frustrated. "Polling shows log-ins are buying it, but the general IRL population smells the BS."

"Losers. No memberships. Not human. No votes."

Roger tapped his pen lightly on the table. He opted not to mention the fact that neither he nor the president had the legal right to vote. Plus, they used a loophole tied to their membership in GA+ that Roger had spent years carefully crafting, to change the laws in order to make it impossible for any serious challengers for the presidency to succeed. Carefully selected districts kept an ineffective opposition just active enough for fundraising. This evangelical Christian faction was never supposed to become a serious challenge. "It is a small, very serious bunch, but they take the living soul as a sacrament," Goodwin said "The truth is, this is not the first time one of them has done this"

This was the sort of thing they tried to keep from the President, who was very fragile about bad news. The last time they told him about the rising Natural Soul movement, he screamed at them to get out of his face.

"Horseshit! Fake! I gave them their soul. For a good price. We gotta show they are safe. No one was hurt, got it? Only certified sanctioned media gets in."

Roger took a deep breath. "There is only one path. It is a bit hypocritical, but..."

The President said nothing. Yanna shook her head and put her hands up trying to signal Roger not to go there.

Roger was days from retiring so he decided to let it fly. "Mister President, I say this as a person who has accepted many sacrifices to work on your staff and to stay alive for that purpose."

Hewit laughed. "Oh, this is rich."

"What the fuck are you trying to say Roger?"

Roger looked at the two people standing in the room with him.

"Tell him," Hewitt leaned back in his chair.

"Yeah, Roger don't be a pussy."

Roger straightened his tie. "Augments. Most of these Natural God people have coolers under their skin. They have surgical eye filters so they can handle the UV. I mean, many of them are at, or close to, 50-P."

Hewitt was the only person under 50-P in this conversation. He was the first to react. "He is saying you need to demonize the Techies."

The President was silent. This could mean he didn't understand.

Roger kept going, "We go after this gunman and his type as not even human; not reflecting God's creation, and say they are a threat to God's plan."

"Yeah, Roger, you know the best part?" The President lit up with his lying grin he got when it occurred to him what to say. "Many people have said it."

Yanna smiled across the table. Hewitt off-camera from the President rolled his eyes.

"They say, 'Mister President, it's true'," The President nodded on the screen. "It's the truth. Many people, they say it."

"Suuuure." Hewitt smiled and stood up. "This is an act of terrorism, so let's start making some arrests and pull some non-profit statuses from subversion churches. Let's get those Techies." Hewitt made finger guns at Yanna and Roger. "Well, present company excluded, of course."

"Great job team!"

The President's screen popped off. Roger watched Hewitt leave.

"Don't forget Canada," Yanna said and walked out.

9

Kai fell asleep playing Citizen Savior. She only earned a few coins for protecting digital citizens. Finding a mass shooter to stop should never be a problem and she wondered sometimes if the program algorithm tracked her bank account and slowed targets whenever she got close to affording Sim-life. She was feeling sleepy so she linked the Cephalochromoscope so she could play the game back later. Her Aver monitored her by the internal ballistocardiogramic sensors she had as implants for this purpose.

Her Aver walked the streets in the game but couldn't find targets.

The game wasn't where the money was now. She knew the game was re-routing the shooters to other players, but that didn't matter because Nick Mayerson was now her coin. The old man's family was powerful, connected, rich, and almost entirely simulated at this point. She only played the game out of habit.

Nick was up, moving around, and he woke her up, although she didn't want to get out of bed. She was supposed to help him, but her body felt heavy. She slept deeper than she expected without a dream circuit. Her mind was a tangled mess of unprogrammed surreal visions. It was not like she never had natural dreams. There were plenty of nights when she didn't have the coin to program. It felt nice to be a guest and not have to pay for the bed. She didn't feel the need to jump when the bed was free.

Nick knocked softly on the door before opening it slightly. He held a Foodle bowl. She could see the steam rising off of it.

"CoffeeISH?"

She pulled her blanket over her uncovered legs and looked at him.

"Oh sorry," he said. "It's a drink, made with almonds. It almost tastes like the real thing."

"The real what?"

"Coffee. A glorious drink from before the jet stream died. It is kinda like an energy Foodle."

Kai was surprised. The Simmies rarely talked about the times before the Second Rev with such affection. It was considered disrespectful to the President. He put the drink on the table beside her bed.

"I should be serving you," she said.

"Nonsense," Nick smiled. "I consider it money well spent to have a guest to serve."

She had only used cups like this in Sim. She hooked her fingers in the handle and lifted the drink up. She was nervous about the heat, butit felt warm and comforting in her mouth and her throat. She liked the sensation, but coughed as her body reacted to it.

"You'll get used to it." He stepped back out of the room and Kai reached down for her pants. Her notifications were filling the menu at the bottom of her vision. She grabbed her Manager and opened the links. When she was logged into Citizen Savior, her Aver was active in the net groups for users who were almost ready to upgrade to GA+.

"The game is never going to let us level up," Kai said out loud, but it was for her Aver. Judging from the comments back and forth that her digital doppelganger had on the message boards, she wasn't alone. It was a little creepy seeing her name and photo involved in these conversations she didn't initiate . The odd thing was it was speaking for her exactly. Word for word it said what she was thinking as she read it. Hours earlier it knew what she would say.

That is why you must focus on Nick. The text appeared on both the Manager and in her Inner-Eye menu. She also knew that the quicker she got him to do the brain-boxing with his family—the so-called 'Great-Upload'—the quicker she would have a life pod of her own.

She felt a burst of energy and the unnatural parts of her body gave her an odd tingle. This is why she avoided energy Foodles. Something Nick couldn't have guessed when he handed her the drink. It wasn't a bad feeling, just strange.

They were close to the three-hundred level where they could play *Night Warrior* or *Citizen Savior* for a living, and get a pod. But the actual membership was more expensive. She needed the old man to play ball.

There was a small bathroom off of her room. Out of habit, she started doing the math in her head, calculating how many credits and coins she would spend on her morning routine. She felt a deep feeling of relief knowing this bathroom was paid for. She only needed to pee every couple of days since she was augmented to retain fluids but she never turned down a free piss.

She sat on the toilet and enjoyed the release. She scrolled the posts and comments that her other self was getting up to. Smartly, her Aver was building relationships with others in the game who were looking to transition soon. Pods were going up for sale as more of the wealthy class were taking part in the Great Upload. Brain-boxing took away their jobs. She wondered if more Janies working their way up had thought this through. There was always the capitalist assumption that someone would always be willing to take the crap jobs and maintain the bottom..

Kai wiped, pulled up her pants, and looked at herself in the mirror. Her bright blue eyes sometimes took attention away from her engineered features. Her dyed hair tips didn't need a brush, just a little water on her fingers as she smoothed out the bed head and made herself presentable. It was a bit of an old-fashioned attitude to worry about her real-life appearance.

She rinsed her fingers and matted her hair down before checking her makeup. The skin on her temple just barely showed the cooling Auggie under her skin. You really had to look for it. Still, she was a 50-P and everyone knew it. Nick Mayerson was a natural who was barely augmented and had treated her like anyone else. She intended to return his respect right up to the moment he uploaded. She had no problem encouraging him to do so, as it was best for him.

She walked out to find him reading the news. She could tell Nick Mayerson worried about his appearance, his greying hair was always combed perfectly, and he was wearing a nice shirt. His Manager was projecting the articles in a holo that simulated the morning paper floating above the table where he was eating Foodle chips and drinking his CoffeeISH.

"Foodle riots in Chicago," he pointed at the article. "Oh, it is supposed to get under 90 degrees overnight. The neighbors are planning some balconies. Parties in the upper levels. I had to bring a jacket once. You want to go?"

Kai laughed at the idea. In her inner eye, she saw a flashing group message that they had both received from Nick's daughter. Kai sat at the table and opened the message. It contained a link that connected them through his Great American pod to a gold-level Heaven trial day.

"You see the message from your daughter? We have to both open it to get the hologram."

Nick reached over to his Manager and selected the message. A small hologram of Miranda Greenstone's online avatar floated over the table.

"Hi Dad, here is your trial link. As realistic as this seems, it is still nothing compared to the lifelike quality of the gold plan. We won't even remember we are in a Sim. Let us know when you are ready."

Miranda faded away, and suddenly, a very white-looking Jesus waved at them to click on a link.

"Don't I have to be in a pod to use the link?"

"That registers the link and sends it to your Pod's server."

"Did she say it was more realistic than this?" He waved at his apartment. There was no sense in debating a naturalist. The heat and tech needed to make survival possible deadened some experiences. The palate and tastebuds being the obvious examples. It was Nick who wanted them to visit the Museum of Human Experience. He was afraid to admit that the most human experience left required the sacrifice.

The hologram of Jesus smiled and then spoke. "Hello, Nick, my son. I see you are hesitating. I am calling to you to join me in the next world. Thanks to the wisdom and business skills of our greatest President, I can offer you something that everyone has always wanted. True peace of mind. With a gold-level membership and proper financial assurance, you can join your loved ones in Heaven. Yes, Heaven. Your technologically designed afterlife. Why leave your mind and spirit open to chance?"

Kai looked at Nick, who was amused by the whole thing. Nick laughed first. Christianity was not the official religion of America until after the Second Revolution, and no one in the support classes paid any attention to it. When the heat kept rising and the coin meant survival, it put all gods into perspective.

"As a philosopher who is old enough to remember religious freedom, I find this sales tactic hilarious."

LEARN MORE

The words floated between them. Only Nick was supposed to select it, as it was his link. The username and password flashed long enough for him to select it. She took advantage of his lack of tech knowledge and used her right eye Ganglion to grab the information. She saved it to her server.

"What now?"

His question brought her back to the moment.

"Give it a shot, Nick. It is just a trial."

"Not convinced yet." Hologram Jesus outstretched his hands, as soft acoustic guitar music played. Kai used her Manager to select Music Ident. The song was called *Pink Houses* as authorized by the Mellencamp estate. A series of pictures floated between them. Images of farms, rivers, and forests all taken during magic hour when the sun was rising or setting, flashed in time to the music. Men stood fishing in the river, families frolicked in the lakes, and a man working a field took out a toothpick and seemed to offer it to Nick. It was a weird moment. The holograms flickered to show women who were in kitchens cleaning, drinking, or cooking something that didn't resemble Foodle. Everyone looked happy.

The voice of the gruff singer sang "But ain't that America, you and me..." His voice faded into the sound of hologram Jesus as he softly spoke. "Nick, I know you remember this America. In Heaven, America is great again. Men are men. They hunt animals in the forests, and they grow food with their own hands. They do what men were designed by our heavenly Father to do. To be strong, to lead the family and country. Women know their roles too. They look beautiful, and every one of them can cook, clean, and be the type of loyal servant we need in a true heaven. Remember, God is always with you."

Kai suddenly felt a tinge of guilt for trying to sign up for this world. Hologram Jesus put out his hand. Kai knew holding that hand opened the link and sent it to the pod. Nick waved off the message and Kai cringed at the look of disgust on his face. He didn't like the sound of it. She didn't either.

"Sounds great, huh?" Kai didn't believe herself.

"Are you kidding me?"

"I may have been young, but I remember the world before the Second Rev. I mean, I voted for the guy the first time."

Kai was a little nervous that he would say he didn't vote for the president after that. Credit ratings and certain privileges in the Sim were known to dry up for those who didn't loudly demonstrate loyalty. Kai wasn't sure she was sold on Heaven for the Living. It seemed more ideologically designed than GA +.

She hated to admit it, but the talking points were popular for a reason. "Nick, it seems to me that part of what makes the Sim so great is that everyone is happy. No shooters, no heat, no need to fill up time with any behavior outside of honoring God, right?"

"I know you get paid if I upload. But, they destroy your body, compost it and soak your brain in hubrizine. It is monstrous."

Kai couldn't deny that she had an interest in convincing him. "Fifty years ago, people were afraid to augment their bodies, and today the human race survives and adapts thanks to our auggies. "

"I thought you were smarter than regurgitating half-baked talking points. You might believe that garbage, but I don't. It is not evolution. It is not living."

"Am I a person?"

"I have treated you like a guest!"

"You also talk to your Manager when it is slow. You even called it baby."

"Habit. Means nothing," Nick was frustrated. "I'm a philosopher. Tell me that my mind is where I exist, and I'll tell you that sucking down Foodle and shitting diarrhea for years on end isn't living."

"...and I will remind you that this life is air conditioned and Foodle supported our experiences in the museum."

"How do you think I would respond to that?"

"Some bullshit about it all being a trick of the mind. And what would I say, Nick?"

Nick sighed and stood up. Outside the window, a few miles away, the brown and red colored dead ocean filled the Horizon as far as his natural eyes could see. "You would say...Free your mind."

"Well?" She leaned back. "You can wait here for the overnight temps to get low enough to hang out on your balconies, but the temps are getting so bad that even the people who can afford a brain box are going crazy before they get there. Half the gen-pop in support services would practically kill themselves to put their mind on ice and forget how they got there."

"You're disgusted by my privilege..." Nick was about to argue with her when the hologram came back on. Jesus was gone, but now the younger middle-aged version of President Supreme pointed at him.

"Hey buddy, you got a moment?"

They were both stunned.

"I get it if Jesus isn't your thing. Move to heaven, and your brain is free. You'll be free to be yourself, just like me. The guy without sin may cast the stone, am I right?" He put out his hand.

Kai gave him a look. "Just a trial. Twenty-four hours. You might as well check out their pizza."

Nick shook his head. "Dirty play."

He shook the virtual president's hand, and his pod buzzed to life behind him.

Kai's server was not able to process such a large amount of data. She couldn't follow Nick. His pod couldn't crunch the data, and she would have to give him a shot, so he didn't lose his mind at all the sensations. She was banking on that. He seemed nervous. He wasn't sure what it felt like, and she knew he was afraid to forget. Getting lost inside a fake world was a fear of his. She understood it was personal fear, a professional hazard for someone who studied philosophy.

He was trembling as she helped him climb into the pod. He could do it himself.He was more capable than most of the Simmers she had supported. She was gentle with the Foodle tubes in his nose. He cringed when she put it in the waste tube.

"They say you forget almost immediately," She patted his shoulder and lowered him down.

"Bullshit," he said with annoyed confidence. "What if it is too much for me to handle?"

Kai held up a syringe with a green liquid. "Hubrizine, to stabilize your Encelphalatraffic."

He fit perfectly into the plastic padded pod bay that was sculpted to his form. She knew many clients who hated the feeling when she shut the lid. His eyes would close, and his mind would drift into the Sim in less than twenty seconds, but his stress could delay the process. She turned his arm over to give him the shot.

"I'll be here when you come back," she said.

Like that, his eyes fluttered and closed. He logged on and her Manager buzzed with a notification. She used her Ganglion to select the message in her inner eye. The message from Miranda Greenstone automatically tipped her seventy-five coins when Nick logged in. The next notification came from her bank. She had crossed to level Three Hundred, with more than enough coins to sign up for a GA + account. She looked at Nick's pod and heard the faint sound of his breathing.

She opened his control panel and saw his usage percentage was below sixty percent, just enough for her to jack his signal and log into GA+. She was legal, but the method of connection was not exactly ethical. She knew it could cost her the contract with Friendlies, but they wouldn't dare risk this client. As long as he didn't log out unexpectedly, no one would ever know. She ran to the kitchen and got a bottle of protein-infused Foodle and chugged it as fast as she could. Because she wouldn't be receiving nutrients, only connecting to the signal, she could fool her mind, but her body would just be wasting away on the floor. She didn't want to wake up depleted but this was a chance to start her new life and she didn't want to miss it.

She laid down next to the pod's server. The stronger the signal, the greater the chances of this working. Nick didn't have much experience. Any Simmer who had done this before would notice the lag when she logged into his signal, but she hopped on unnoticed.

The pod's firewall popped up on her Manager, and it told her that this stream was blocked. She asked for the override and copied the log-in she had stolen earlier. If she jumped the signal directly to the HFL server it would fry the augments near her skull and cause an aneurysm. This was part of the brain activity that the Hubrizine protected users from. She wished the Gold-plan salesman had sent more than one shot.

She could log into Great America Plus and join the Sim in real time. It was also Tuesday online, and she would have a safe twenty hours to herself. She knew would log out hungry and in a puddle of her own waste, but she couldn't pass this up.

She sent the date to her Aver who sent her links to the friends she had made in the Sim. In a matter of minutes she would be in the Los Angeles Sim.

She laid a towel under her real body so there would be less to clean up and looked up at the ceiling. She started her countdown.

"Ten, nine, eight..."

———

Nick wiped the grease off his fingers and looked out at the ocean. There were three French fries left on the plate. His plate of carne asada was history. His gut felt a little heavy. He thought maybe he should've stopped earlier, but he couldn't remember the last time he had eaten anything that tasted that delicious. The fries had been cooked in truffle oil. The flavor was so strong he licked his bottom lip and sensed it. He even smelled the soft rosemary spices on his fingers.

The Pacific Ocean was only a short walk away from him across the sand, and it distracted him from his food. The crashing blue waves rolled in over and over as they always did. He didn't understand why, but it looked more beautiful than ever. The blue of the water was soft and alive. The air carried a soft mist from the ocean that smelled heavenly.

Lisa appeared out of the water. Her two-piece bathing suit matched her tan and hugged her perfect hourglass curves. In the distance, she looked nude.

His wife eclipsed the beauty around her. Certainly, he was biased. He also thought she was the smartest, most compassionate, and hilarious person alive. Her long dark hair was tied in a messy knot behind her head. She walked out of the water and stopped to grab a towel laying on the sand. She dried herself off slowly. He didn't need to think twice. He stood up and made his way over to her. He didn't run to her, but he was quick about it. When he got up to her, she was laying in a sexy pose on the towel and patted for him to join her.

Nick sat on the towel and wondered what this angel sent from heaven saw in him. As he sat, he felt the slight radiant warmth of the sand under the towel. He looked into her sunglasses. He was there in the reflection. He saw himself for just a moment before she pulled them off. That was strange. He didn't know why, but a part of him didn't expect to look so young. He didn't know why, but it felt wrong.

"Do you want to swim?" Her eyes were as blue as the ocean, speckled with diamond-bright accents. In moments like this, he was reminded how breathtaking she was.

"Something wrong, Nick?"

He looked around at the people playing on the beach. A moment ago they seemed closer, but now he felt like they were almost alone on the beach.

"No, sweetheart. Nothing is wrong."

Lisa grabbed his shirt and pulled him nearer. Nothing was sexier than a lover who needed you closer. She gently kissed him. Her hand slid to the back of his neck, making sure he had no escape from her kiss. He melted into it, and for a moment the universe disappeared. Only her lips and their bodies melted together.

She pushed her lips to his neck. "Can we go home?"

The words were spoken on his skin, and he felt them in his toes.

Kai wore an Asian Sim-skin made popular in pre-revolution K-pop night-clubs. Her look changed to match her Sims-sync beat, and the colors in her hair changed with the beat of the music. As she danced the Ganglion in her operated as it would in real life. She scanned the crowd, and usernames popped up. It was impossible to tell who was a bot, or who was living Sim-jacked into a pod. There were clubs like this back home in the towers. The music was DJ'ed by a bot programmed by a long-dead and brain-boxed MC. It was a layered hybrid of early 20th-century hip-hop and modern Aug-hop. The old-school song played inside the club, fading in and out while the pounding rhythm internally bounced off the augments near her ear. It was music designed for the deaf, and there was nothing like the beat rattling your bones. The dance floor was called the cluster, a mass of bodies colliding that would batter natural bodies.

Kai danced, but something was off. There was no pain, no level of fear mixing with the power of the beat. The simulation was trying to replicate the feeling but it felt fluffy and safe. A mix of fancy dresses, hot numbers, and non-gendered clothes of style spun around her. As she moved through the crowd, players and crawlers would scan her code and tip her coins just for looking hot.

The clubs in the towers were populated by techies and support class Janies blowing off steam after hours spent cleaning out Foodle ports and brushing clean waste tubes. These clubs were filled with Simmers who benefitted from that toil and who lived in a climate-controlled reality where the weather was always perfect. In the towers, they needed the Augs to live. No one was happy to have them, but here, they tried to replicate that feeling.

There was a moment on the dance floor when a woman rubbed against her hip, it was hot. She turned to sync and got her username. The mocha-skinned woman had obvious cooling augments under her temple and it stopped Kai. No one back home would choose to wear that style of augment so openly. Kai wondered if this woman was even a person of color.

The music was a remix of an early-century hip-hop song that her Ganglion identified as a song called *'Make the hood go crazy.'* Kai turned her internal volume down and listened to the crowd stomp and breathe heavily. Her Sim body required the illusion of breath, closer to that of a natural human, so she was surprised how quickly she got tired dancing. It was something else.

She turned down offers to dance all night. Kai walked to the bar. She wasn't prepared for how fake everything would feel. Her brain kept trying to convince her it was real. The floor was sticky, the air humid. The realism was down to details like the puddle left by the open spot on the bar from the melted ice and condensation. Kai felt the tepid water with her finger. It felt real but a part of her was trying to remind her that it was a Sim.

She was glad to know that clubs, however sterile, existed here. Great America Sims were supposed to be wholesome, family affairs. This network was coded after the revolution when America was returning to its values as the President told them they would. In the real world, it was "drill baby, drill," big trucks with big gun racks, and bigger gas tanks. It was illegal to admit the truth that anyone in the support class experienced daily. Great American values didn't function with global ecology. So the Sim was the solution.

Kai dreamed of living in this world her whole life and had always wanted to. She spent the day checking out the city. It looked like LA, but she almost felt cold. The streets were clean, and traffic moved. The sky was blue. There was an odd feeling that the skyline disappeared when she had her back to it. She never forgot she was in a Sim, but she knew that when she was on a stronger, legal signal, she just might.

There were stores everywhere, and everything cost real-life coins. The banks didn't care that she was on a hacked signal. Her money was still good. She was still able to earn. Knowing she was online now, her Aver was hard at work playing the game, looking for coin.

She got ice cream for lunch. She had heard of it but never had any. It reminded her of Almond Foodle left in a freeze-box. She savored every bite but wanted to lie down after eating it. She needed a home in the Sim. She wanted to live near the ground, which would have been impossible in the real world. She knew there were Sim homes that she could share with thousands who rented a pocket reality in GA +.

The house was small but bigger than any Conapt back home. It was in a quiet neighborhood on Francisco Street. It had fading yellow paint and two stories. After she dropped the coin, she sat on the front step and looked out at the school across the street. Children came out at 3:15 p.m. on the dot, running to waiting parents, whom she didn't see arrive. She wasn't sure the children or the parents were real. They could've just been flavor for the neighborhood. Simulated children had become the only substitute for people who insisted on succumbing to that instinct despite the state of the planet.

All the children were smiling and perfect. None of them misbehaved or got angry about anything and they all grew up to be perfect citizens who respected the President.

Kai watched a little girl with a backpack bigger than she was drag a President Supreme lunch box to her waiting mother. Most children here were parented by Simmy-sitters.

Her house was perfect. She would have to teach herself how to cook and live Great America style. The whole day felt uncomfortable until she got to the club. She had to know, was all of Great America Plus like this? She watched the people dancing. It all looked safe and comfortable. Could she find a party? You had to dig, hack some codes, and find the dark corners of the Sim, but it was there.

A man sitting at the bar turned his chair around to look at her. He was handsome if you were into that kinda thing. Kai's dating experience was almost entirely digital, and nothing this realistic.

"Hey there, your first time?"

Kai was taken aback. "Uhh, no."

"Come on Kai, your user history is available. Even if it wasn't..."

"I look obvious?"

He nodded. "I can tell when I see tourists."

"I'm not a tourist, I just leveled up."

"Sure, thing honey. However much you are getting paid. I looked at your profile. Pretty, my type if you are looking for a sponsor..."

Kai rolled her eyes and walked out to the dance floor. She used her server to crank up the volume and disappeared into the storm of bodies.

———

It was her hand on his back that first woke him up. The sheets were wet with his sweat, and hers. As he drifted awake, he felt her getting closer. She spooned up against his back. He felt the familiar shape of her body against him. She always thought their bodies were crafted by the universe to fit snugly together. Her nose nestled behind his left ear. He listened to her breath softly. It woke him faster than any alarm.

"Morning," Lisa whispered.

The sun rose outside their window. The birds were singing to greet the day. He didn't remember where he left his clothes. He thought about getting up and making Lisa breakfast. She was simple. She liked toast and green tea. Her body held him to the bed with the force of gravity.

"What does a wife around here have to do to get some breakfast in bed?"

"I want to, but..." Nick rolled over just enough to see her smile. She kissed his forehead.

"It has been twenty-four hours, baby," She whispered before giving him a soft kiss.

"It's been what?"

"Get up, get me some breakfast. Trust me, it will feel better if you are in the other room."

He gripped her hand. "What is wrong, Lisa?"

"Too late," She closed her eyes. "Come back to me, another day. Forever."

The world shook. Earthquake is not a strong enough word. It was like being inside a bottle that was being shaken by a gorilla. Instinctively, Nick reached out for Lisa. He had to keep her safe. He braced for the ceiling to come crashing down on them, for the house to fall out from under him. He screamed when he reached for her and she wasn't there. Suddenly, the cool morning air slipped away from him, like God had sucked it away in giant straw. The sun glowed orange and impossibly bright.

Lisa was gone. The warm air surrounded him like a hug from an oven coil. A young woman with strange colored hair pulled the tubes from his nose. Another tube moved painfully inside of him as he thrashed, and she pulled it from his ass.

"Nick! Nick!" She pleaded.

He felt the tube scrape his colon even as the feeling of his sweet Lisa's breath echoed like a burn on his skin.

"Lisa!" Nick screamed and reached out. He only found a face he didn't know.

"Mister Mayerson! The Trial is over. You're back."

He breathed the hot air. A day ago it didn't feel hot, it felt normal. He looked at the young techie. A name floated just beyond him. He knew her.

"It's me, your Janie Kai."

Then the reality came back to him like being dunked in cold water. Kai, the pod, the trial for Heaven. He had forgotten it all. He believed every minute of it. Now he was back in the burning hot apartment in the tower. He had returned to the burning earth, and his heart broke into a thousand pieces. He sobbed, unable to control the tears. He felt Kai awkwardly patting his shoulder.

"It's okay, okay."

It most certainly wasn't.

10

THE BREEZE WAS STRONG enough to cause ripples in the swimming pool. Just beyond the deck of the resort, the ocean was reaching high tide. Roger was in the pool dunking their grandchild Jamie for the fourth time. The boy's laughter was impossible to ignore but Roger hardly ever got tired. Four generations of Miranda Greenstone's family were gathered at the pool.

Her Father, Nick Mayerson, came around the pool, wearing the faded Cal-Berkeley shirt he had worn in the family photo taken on the favorite day of her childhood. They were all gathered at the beach house near Torrey Pines. She spent almost the whole day in the waves. Her father had not aged a day, and her mother Lisa sat with her legs in the pool, her dress pulled up to stay dry. The grandkids kept playfully spritzing her. She loved every moment.

Nick sat in the lounge chair and looked up at the clear blue sky. One cloud hung in the perfect spot to block the sun.

"Hey Dad," She pointed at the cooler and the green Rolling Rock bottle waiting for him.

"Sure, you don't want a real beer?"

"Real enough," Nick used the edge of the chair to pop the bottle cap. They both laughed as Roger held his grandson by his feet trying to shake change out of his pockets. "There against all your doubt is a happy great-grandson." Miranda leaned her iced tea to click with his beer bottle—a simple toast.

Nick gulped his beer. He sighed with a deep satisfaction that seemed off. She couldn't quite place it.

"My doubt?" He was confused.

"Yeah, Debbie downer." They didn't argue as far back as the birth of her children. Her father was so convinced that the world was doomed, he shamed her for even the notion of having children. All of this happened before the Second Revolution freed America from fear. It was fuzzy, but she remembered the arguments. It seemed petty now, sitting here.

"I never doubted Jamie, I love the boy."

Miranda was about to argue with him and say that was not the point, then she looked at the sky beyond him. The air was perfect, and the temperature was fine. Her father's dire warnings seemed more ridiculous than ever. He didn't vote for President Supreme, and said he would never support him, but look at the world he built.

Nick Mayerson leaned back and relaxed under the shade of an umbrella and watched the family play. The piano player ended the song she was softly playing. Everyone around the pool clapped. Miranda never looked over before, but the musician disappeared for a moment, and then a hologram of Elton John shimmered to life and started to play a soft version of *Don't Go Breaking My Heart.*

An awkward crowd gathered around the piano and hologram Elton John welcomed the crowd. A small dance was breaking out by the pool.

Lisa Harris Mayerson stood up, tipping her sun hat up. She smiled and pointed at the piano. "Elton John!"

"Well, sort of, I guess," said the hologram.

"Close enough." Nick Mayerson got up and did a little dance with his wife. It was embarrassing and cute at the same time just like parents are supposed to be.

Miranda stood up and walked away from the group to look at the ocean. She had looked at it her whole life but something felt different in this moment. The breeze felt salty, there was a smell of life. She closed her eyes and listened to the waves roll. She felt the hand on her shoulder. She didn't have to look to know it was Roger.

He looked young and full of energy. A part of her knew that the President worked him to death, so why did he look so young? He looked better than she remembered, with a jawline that rivaled Brad Pitt. She hadn't married Roger for his looks. He was handsome enough, but he was going places when she was at Yale. Now, a receding hairline and the start of a belly were starting to show, but more importantly, Roger Greenstone still had drive and ambition and nothing was hotter to a young Miranda.

"Something isn't right?" She whispered.

Roger laughed and looked around. "It is pretty perfect around here."

Miranda sighed. Why couldn't she just be happy? It was just beyond her. A huge part of her wanted to accept it all, and she didn't know wha,t but something was off. She turned back to see her father dancing. He seemed to accept all this without question.

"Twenty-four hours," Roger said flatly as he rubbed the small of her back.

"What?" Miranda leaned against the deck railing.

"Your trial is up."

"My trial?" The world began to shake, Miranda closed her eyes and held on to the railing. "What is happening?"

She was seconds from screaming, but it never left her throat. The sky faded; the resort blew away like a sandcastle in a hurricane. The cool air melted into a soupy thick heat. Miranda felt like she was choking and ejected the tube from her mouth with a gut-wrenching heave. A person sat over her holding the tube. She felt confused.

What happened to the world? It was just here. Where was Dad? Mom? Roger, the kids...Roger is the person she needed at this moment. Her arms gripped the person standing over her. They wore a uniform, and a name tag read "Holly."

"It's fine Ms. Greenstone, I'm here."

"Roger? Oh god, Roger?"

She pleaded and her eyes scanned the room. It looked less familiar than the resort did. She saw a family photo on the wall. Her family. She looked at Holly. She looked like a woman but her skin was off slightly. Something glowed and flashed under the flesh on her temple. The longer Miranda stared into her eyes -- they were green but they made a tiny buzz—and the pupils were technology.

"It's me, Holly."

This Holly seemed to expect Miranda to know her, and in something near to a memory she knew a Holly existed, but she couldn't find her. She didn't want to know. She wanted to be back at the resort. She wanted to hear *Rocketman* and to dance with her father. *What was this bullshit?*

Her mind rejected it even as her eyes lowered to Roger's life pod. Holly gently pulled the waste tube out of her backside, lifted her shorts, and guided her off the pod toward the couch. There was no dignity left to her, but Holly acted as if this was normal. It took a moment, but now she remembered Holly, her Janie. It was her job to care for Miranda.

"Trial…" Miranda whispered. She tried to admit to herself what it was. Her 24-hour trial of Heaven for The Living. She had to admit to herself that was what it was. Something inside her was rejecting all this. The war over what was reality was taking place inside her.

"How was it?" Holly asked as she wiped the sweat off her brow. It was at that moment that Miranda noticed the heat in their apartment high above Silver Springs. She heard the AC working to cool the room. Hard to deny.

"Wow, just wow." Miranda laughed and looked around. She had forgotten it all. Just twenty-four hours. She had hints; her father not acting like himself, her mother being there, as just a flat recreation based on her social media. Twenty-four hours and she forgot about the life-pods, hotboxes, all of it. It was America as it was and always meant to be. God bless America, and God bless President Supreme.

"Amazing, I never questioned…it felt more than just real." She needed her father. The real Nick Mayerson would make a world that felt like home. He deserved it. She needed to make that happen. She smiled at Holly. "I believed."

Kai looked at her hand and moved her fingers. There was a lag between having the thought and the movement.. It was close to imperceptible, but from the moment she logged out of Great America, a full hour before Nick Mayerson's Heaven trial ended, it continued. She hoped her mind and tech would sync back up soon.

Nick Mayerson was not doing any better, he sat on his couch, rocking for the better part of the last twenty minutes wrapped in a blanket saying the name "Lisa" over and over. She assumed that was the wife in the old pictures and video frames around the Conapt. Kai watched the sweat form on his brow and she could smell it. She should've taken his blanket but neither of them was in any shape to interact.

Kai's mind and body were out of whack. She had spent more than 22 hours jacked into an illegal world, and her body had acclimated to it. She knew what she needed, but leaving the tower was not possible. Sauce would fix her up quickly. For Nats and Normies, it regulated body temperature. For a 50-P like herself, after a moment of surfing a great cosmic wave, when the wave crashed it soaked into the shore all the crossed wires were straight as the edge of a ruler.

Deep breaths and hand squeezes were the best she could do.

I have to get back there, she thought, but the text also appeared in the chat window with her Aver.

You have to convince him.

Kai looked at the scared-looking old man. She saw the words in her inner eye, and used the Ganglion to move it out of her menu. She knew what had to be done. She grabbed a washcloth and ran it under cold water in the kitchen. She bumped into a chair on her way back to the living room. If he was watching her, Nick may have questioned her sync.

She sat on the couch with him. She wiped his brow. He let out a sigh and looked at her. She expected fear, but that wasn't it. It was confusion.

"How was it?"

"Fuck…"

Kai laughed. She could almost see the hooks in his skin pulling him in. Something happened in that Sim that he wanted to get back to.

"It was her, I felt her, I tasted her," he touched his lips. "It was her."

It wasn't, Kai thought, but that was the last thing she was going to say. Kai nodded and smiled. She understood. She wanted her house on Francisco Street to be a real house. She knew it was a Sim, and she could see Nick Mayerson, who was more of a Nat and a Luddite, had been fooled. She knew his mind accepted it. A small part of her felt guilty watching his walls crumble. He wanted to tell her that she was the lie, that this world was fake. He believed it too.

She had spent her whole life sweating out hotboxes and augmenting her body just to keep alive. She deserved to free her mind, and if he was the key…

"Yes, Nick, it was her. You can give up this…", she hesitated, "…this illusion."

"This Illusion?"

"Plato believed there were forms of reality that consisted of the many…"

"…and the one. You've been reading, my dear."

Kai shrugged. "Is your reality any less real? Did you taste her? What can be more real than love? I see it on your face. Defining reality has been a struggle since Plato, but you know she exists, and your love for her is more real than all this. You of all people know, Nick. It is your life's work to create a reality."

Nick smiled and slowly licked his bottom lip. He didn't say anything, but Kai knew…She had him.

11

THE LAG WAS NOT getting better. Kai tried to go about her day. She prepared CoffeeISH and Foodle for Nick who just stared out the window silently while his drinks became lukewarm. He was her job, and technically she was on the clock. He was Sim-wrecked. His mind was still anchored to the Sim, and it was her job to straighten him out, snap a finger in his face, and ground him. Or was it? She needed him to ascend to the great upload, and maybe this was the best way.

Kai wasn't exactly in a better place. It was hard to accept reality when your brain and technology were off. Nick wasn't even looking at her, so she logged on to socials. It was like she never left. Her name and her picture were there for conversations about the games, influencers, and new augments on the market. She scrolled until she saw the Citizen Savior link and entered the game.

A message popped up from her Aver: *Would you like to play?* She was hunting a shooter in an early 21st-century shopping mall. She hadn't taken out a Lone Wolf in sixteen hours of gameplay. Too busy chatting up message boards inside the Sim and flooding socials with details of the house on Franciso street.

Kai didn't remember being this open about her personal details. Kai wanted to play, she wanted to earn money, and that had not been a concern of her Aver. It was supposed to think like her. She wanted to play, but every movement was delayed; on and offline. She tested her sync by smacking the counter and had to wait three seconds to hear the sound. When it's about your tether to reality, three seconds is enough to create madness for anyone.

She closed the game. The illegal Sim worked in the moment, but now it was busting her sync, causing a headache, and giving her a feeling like a screw twisting in the back of her skull.

She needed Sauce. Chemical 6-00-6 cut and modified for street sales. It was easy to come by in the city if you knew the right people, and she did. The problem was she was in Santa Ana and she didn't have any connections south of the 405.

Santa Ana is north of the 405. The text appeared in her menu, and she understood the point her Aver was trying to make. It annoyed her to have her AI correct her thoughts. There it was. Her own Aver thought it was smarter than her. It happens. She started to wonder if she had sabotaged her Aver. Was she losing coin in the game while the program was off?

"Fuck off," Kai turned to Nick on the couch, and he didn't seem to think she was talking to him. He didn't react. "Hey, Nick? Are we north of the 405 here?"

Nick, didn't respond. Didn't even turn to look at her. She would have to deal with that, but right now she just needed a little something to get right.

Kai pulled up the map and was surprised how much of Orange County was north of parts of the LA metro area and Long Beach.

"Well, shit," Kai whispered as she waited for her Aver to give an "I told you so." Perhaps they were not so linked after all. It didn't matter. The point, the problem, the need at hand was that they were too far south for any pushers she knew.

She opened an empty post on a social for Janies in South Bay, thinking Long Beach was close enough. She couldn't just post and ask for Sauce.

LA Janie stationed in Santa Ana looking to score some 6—paying in net-based Kibble so come to Daddy, please.

She waited. Forty generated replies appeared in her inbox for expensive pharmacy shops that would sell watered-down medical grade 6-00-6. She needed to take a dose that would last and keep her baseline if she got the chance to stream again. Finally, after weeding through several messages offering her Kibble for just opening the text, she found the first real offer.

Thorton Park—Twenty minutes. First half transferred in thirty seconds or no deal.

It was expensive, but the seller had a verified account. Traceable. Kai transferred the money without thinking and got the verification with a pin to follow to the park.

"I'll be back in an hour," she told Nick who didn't notice her grabbing her bag or heading to the door. As she stepped into the hall, she thought she heard Nick saying goodbye, but she couldn't be sure it was an echo. The pin sent directions directly to her inner eye lens. Sky Tram was due at the roof port on the next building across the sky bridge in fifteen minutes. She pulled off her Gogs and dust scarf before stepping out of the elevator onto the Skybridge. The midday sun was burning with intense UV on the eastern horizon in the direction she was looking for the SkyMetro. The station was deserted, and she connected to the server to find arrivals and departures. The port played a trippy Aug-Hop song on her server and showed the distance of the tram in her menu. Eight minutes. She looked out over the sprawl to the east, the towers seemed to sway, but she knew that was her lag.

The hot box below was between dust-offs, but she could see the low sand clouds gathering to the east. Kai leaned on the railing and watched for the tram when a baseball-sized Plugger flew over her shoulder and scanned her eyes, making contact with her augments. *"Ride Sky Metro on us. Just enjoy this short ad."* The plugger spoke in the voice of Kai's favorite influencer Lou-doll. *"Come on Kai, it is an important message and you'll save some coin baby girl."*

The button floated in her vision, and using her Ganglion she accepted the ad. The sounds of the sky above Orange County faded out. There was a drum roll and the sound of footsteps. The video faded in as it played on her inner eye. It was still subject to her lag but the video was suddenly all she could see. She gripped the railing as she felt the wind push her around.

The video showed a slim, young version of President Supreme. He had not even looked like before he was first elected. He waved and a few steps behind him the other members of the political party waved in his wake.

"It's your favorite President!" a booming voice called out as the orange-skinned man reached the podium. It was clear as a bell. The volume was louder, and the video was in perfect sync. That inspired a moment of paranoid wondering.

"Hey there proud Americans, can you believe it? We did it! Our records show you have recently upgraded to our glorious, beautiful Great America + Sim world. Of course, we know that in GA Plus, America is as great and wonderful as our founding fathers intended. But in order to maintain that American dream we must maintain the business of the real world. The Lib-tards are at it again. They don't value your hard work, and they are indoctrinating the children through schools with filthy old-world, long-thought-dead socialist and communist doctrines. They will take away your guns leaving you a surefire target for Lone Wolf gunmen and force your children to encourage so-called gender affirmations. <Kai> Join us with a donation to the Party."

The video faded and she saw the Tram getting closer. The Plugger flashed as it paid her fare.

"What level would you like to donate to make sure your boys grow up to be men, and girls grow up to be women?" The President's voice seemed automated. She felt watched and judged. Her citizen rating would take a hit, but she was about to blow a bunch of coin.

Kai clicked the *Maybe Another Day* tab and the Plugger imitated a sad sound as it floated away looking for someone else. The tram doors opened and a pair of Janies returning from a shopping trip nodded at her as they stepped off. She got in the tram, and since she only needed to go to two stops she didn't even sit down. It was closer to noon, so there were plenty of empty seats but it was just easier to stay on her feet. The ads in the windows scrambled, each targeting one of her interests. She closed her eyes and waited for her stop.

As they got closer the tram had to lower a bit and her eyes got wide as she saw the 40-acre park with a pond and several play structures on a raised platform to take advantage of the thinner and cooler air. There were a couple of trails and you could see a few people walking but as they got closer the playground equipment was rusted and the water in the pond was brown and stagnant.

Parks were a luxury of Sim-worlds, anyone with the time and resources didn't go to what most people called Stick-Parks, which could only be raised so high, and most still died out. Only one person waited at the tram stop. Kai got off, and the man stood by a shopping cart that appeared to be filled with clothes and a dirty unrolled sleeping bag. This man wasn't poor or homeless. He was using that stuff as a cover for his stock.

Now arriving at your pinned destination.

Kai felt a bit of remorse as she stepped on the park platform. They were alone, no one else in sight. She was putting a lot of trust in this person. The Pusher wore a dirty grey sweat-suit, likely a part of the outfit meant to make him appear homeless. No one wanted to see or acknowledge the homeless. It was like being invisible.

"Kai?" He asked, his voice felt distant. She saw the glassy look before. She relaxed a little knowing he was a Phantom. His actions were driven by programming. He had been born natural but chose upgrade after upgrade until...

"That's me."

She guessed he was 70-P. His actual mind was directing his virtual body in GA +, while his Aver was programmed to do the grunt work of pushing

Sauce in the park. His eyes were completely mechanical, and his body moved awkwardly.

"We doing business?" The Phantom asked

"I don't want Foodle powder pills, I need pure sauce."

"Why do you think I wanted a down payment? You have the coin, I have the pills."

The Phantom held up a baggy that had about two dozen white tablets. "It will fix your sync which is good because you sound like a fucking retard."

Kai put out her hand. The Phantom shook his head. "Coin first, then get your ass home because you're going to be straight pizzled out of your brain for six hours."

"How pizzled are we talking?"

He looked her over. "Looks like you got some of your birthday suit left, but these babies will do a number on your wetware connects and you might feel a little pizz or you might see flying monkeys coming out of your ass. Who's to say?"

Kai made the payment.

"Keep my number sweetheart," the phantom said as he put the bag in her hand.

"Not a chance, but thanks for the Sauce, Doc."

The Phantom pointed at the coming metro. She didn't need to be asked twice. For the first time in close to an hour, she remembered her client. Nick Mayerson had the key to her future. The Metro approached, and she knew she had to get her thoughts back on him.

12

THEY HAD TO FLY overnight, but that was common these days. After a certain weight, planes were too heavy to take flight in the heat. They already had to take a Hypertube underground trolley to a York, Pennsylvania, airstrip where air was dense enough for a flight out of the storm zone that was battering the east coast. The Michelle Shirley Storm Prediction Center showed no clear skies over Dulles for a week. If Roger Greenstone was going to get to Canada, he had to take the train and wait for the night to cool down.

During the flight, Roger got more than a dozen messages from his speech-bots with talking points for the media. It might not exactly be how he handled things on the ground, but it helped him.

Miranda had not messaged him since she did her Heaven trial. He had a feeling about how it went. Since the last three updates of the Heaven operating systems, the immersion was so good that most people logging off their free trials were unwilling to accept reality itself, and were desperate to get back inside. Of course, it would have to feel that way if they wanted people to agree to give up their bodies.

The flight attendant signaled his server that they were making their approach. He saw the Secret Service agents unbuckling their belts. The sun poked up from the east over Canada. They weren't supposed to have any authority here, but since northern Saskatchewan and Manitoba became the breadbasket of the western world, Canada had given up control in exchange for funding, which they used for climate crisis construction and Sim research.

The pink and purple fields of high-yield Amaranth rolled under them as the plane made its descent.

Thanks to his role at the White House, he knew the state of affairs in the rest of the world. Although President Supreme had declared that whatever happened internationally didn't matter as long as he made America great again. Roger never argued as most people didn't care about the rest of the world anyway.

He always got nervous during landing and take-off. When he was still young and the skies were crowded, he didn't think much about it. Flight in and out of the hotbox now was much more difficult. Most pilots lived in Sims and piloted Phantom. It didn't help him relax to think his life and limb were basically part of a pilot's video game. Some pilots trained entirely on Sim, and he had been assured often that the planes could do much of the work automatically, just like an Auto-Auto.

The plane bounced a bit as they landed on the tarmac and there was a collective sigh as the air brakes slowed them to a taxi.

"We have less than an hour before the air pressure grounds us here till nighttime," Walter Nelson, his mostly technologically altered secret service agent said, as he unbuckled. "Should we stay packed on the plane or get rooms?"

Roger sighed. He wanted to get this done quickly, but he wasn't hopeful. He looked out the window and the fields were yellow and dry. The fields were grown as close as twenty feet to the runway. In the air, robotic farm drones dropped seeds and recycled water that they pulled out of the humidity to mist the fields. That warm, sticky air just couldn't grow anything else anymore. The heat and the extinction of bees had led to a near-global collapse of agriculture, but it was the perfect time for humanity to adapt. Especially when those with the financial means to could free their minds.

Human farmhands imported from various countries that had descended into chaos when the water dried up were still needed to pick the sensitive crop before it was transported south to the factories that made Foodle. It was those ungrateful bastards that were the reason he was here. Back home, they would have already died fighting over the last drops of water.

Roger scanned the farms he could see from his window. He searched his files and pulled the data up in his inner eye. He had to scroll a little, but the information he worried about was there. The planting season was months ago. From the look of things, he had a sinking feeling that the crop failed, and this was a second attempt.

"I think we need rooms," he said, "but tell everyone to expect wheels up as soon as the fucker sets."

Walter nodded and signaled his team to be the first off the plane. Roger waited for them to give him a go and when they did he exited the plane. He expected the air to be cooler, but it wasn't. It was just as muggy and thick as DC. The dawn air still held some radiant energy from the day before.

A welcoming committee from the Manitoba Farm Board stood waiting just inside the airport doors, flanked by both Canadian and American flags. Eighty-five percent of the farms in this province were purchased by American protein interests. The flags made him laugh but he thought, "Hey, let them do their ritual."

He accessed his Ganglion and scanned the man walking toward him. *Shaun Sawyer, Manitoba Trade Council.* The man looked uncomfortable in his suit. As he got closer Roger could tell this man was a Nat, and likely a third-generation farmer who was more comfortable in the fields. He had tried to comb his white hair, but he had a faint hat-head that circled his hair, matching up with a hat-induced tan line.

As he walked toward him, Roger saw a text pop up from Miranda: *It was incredible, we have got to convince Dad! Go to him if you have to.*

Roger realized in that moment he might have to go to California. There was little he could do to get out of it now. One thing for sure, he didn't have time for this shit he was dealing with.

"Mister Greenstone, welcome to Manitoba I am trade minister Sawyer. If you would follow me."

Roger leaned back to Walter and whispered. "Cancel the rooms." He turned back to Sawyer and shook his head. "Right here is good."

Sawyer wiped the sweat off his brow. "We have a meeting room here at the airport. It is more comfortable."

"I don't want to be comfortable, Mister Sawyer. I want to be on my plane heading back to DC to give the President the good news."

"The good news?" Sawyer looked at Roger's advisors. his team, and even the Secret Service agents. He was wondering if Roger was serious. He didn't say anything. He didn't have to.

"I'm not kidding," Roger continued. "We spend a lot of the American GDP on your land under the impression that it is cool enough to grow Foodle base, so it should be cool enough to have a little chat about why your yield is dipping."

"Sure, right here. Should I get chairs brought out?"

Roger shook his head. "Why the fuck is your yield dropping? We have riots over Foodle already. Your farms are not delivering. What is the goddamn problem?"

"We all live on the same planet, Mister Greenstone," Sawyer was making a subtle insult. He knew damn well that most people lived their lives in the Sim.

"I am not a meteorologist," Roger said. "I am not sure why I would need to be."

Sawyer was angry, but he took the time to consider his next words. "There is only so much fresh water, and the heat domes are moving further north every season."

"You told us this crop could adapt."

Swayer was uncomfortable and tried to disarm the moment with a smile. "Sir, I prepared a presentation. If we could step inside. We have donuts, they're taro-based but..."

"Stop, just stop." Roger waved at Sawyer to follow him. "Walk with me, Sawyer."

The man looked at his advisors, nervous about walking alone with the White House Chief of Staff. Roger understood so he smiled this time and waved the white-haired older official to follow him. Sawyer loosened his tie, took off his suitcoat, and gave it to one of his aids.

Roger waited until they were out of earshot of anyone else. "Keep your voice low Mister Sawyer. I want this conversation to be just between us."

Sawyer nodded. "Does this mean I can be brutally honest, Mister Green-stone?"

"Call me Roger, and that is the idea. The President wants me swinging my dick around you understand." Roger didn't know if Sawyer believed that the anger was just for show.

Sawyer looked at him compassionately for just a moment. "I am sorry to be the one to tell you all this Roger, but we have been sending warnings for a few seasons now. Crops are failing. Some tracts of land we have seeded and re-seeded but the growth is below yield in thirty percent of the fields, and another twenty percent are simply dead."

Roger closed his eyes for a moment. That was easy math to do, but hard to accept. Fifty percent output was not enough to create Foodle for those living in the Sim, let alone those in the support class. Their national reserves in Colorado would only last six months. He knew how the president responded to news like this: He didn't. "*Fake news and lies.*" He would expect some kind of technological bailout.

In the old days, the President's staff joked that he deployed the Sims to fool the population, much like he swirled his hair around his head to try and fool the public he wasn't bald. There was no escape from the truth this time.

"Can you move operations north?"

"We have tried."

"Of course, you did."

"The bees were key pollinators. We can't match with technology the skill that they spread the seeds..."

"Bees? Motherfucking bees," Roger shook his head in disbelief.

"They are important, they play a key..."

"There are thousands and thousands of bee species," Roger shrugged.

"There were. Now...the plants and the bees spent millions of years evolving together. Your robots are programmed by smart people in the labs, but not millions of years of evolution smart."

"Fucking bees," Roger whispered as he thought about his grandmother's house. Her yard was filled with flowers. She loved working out there. When they were little, it was scary to walk to her front door through a gauntlet of bees. That was until she hung a yellow bottle from the front porch. He never knew how it worked, but the bees got inside and died. He didn't even remember seeing the bees again around her door after that. At the time, he was pretty happy to never see those bees again.

"We want your contracts, Roger, but you'll have to rely on someone else."

Roger let out a nervous laugh. "Who?" Alaska had closed its borders, and the northern regions of Russia were a constant warzone of various armies that had moved north to escape the heat. The President was more than happy to let them all duke it out as long as they were able to keep the Sims on and Foodle flowing.

"You know what is ironic?" All the nervous energy was gone from Sawyer. "The Aztecs offered Amaranth to the gods..."

Roger didn't need him to finish that thought. "Just grow what you can." He snapped his finger and Agent Nelson walked over to him. He couldn't fuck around. He and his family needed to leave the party before things got worse.

"Sir?" He looked at Roger, but he could tell instantly Nelson was phantomed.

"No, absolutely not. No Avers right now. I need the real Walter here, not some phantom bullshit."

Roger waited as Walter closed his eyes. When he opened them, his phantom was gone, and the real Agent Nelson was back. It was something you always had to consider when working with a 70-P.

"Wheels up in fifteen minutes. Tell that fucking tower we need to get to cruising before the sun starts climbing."

He nods. "I'll let the White House know..."

Roger shook his head, "Tell the crew we are heading to California. We have a mission, highest-security clearance, Coms black-out, so that means keep your traps shut. We will be back in DC on the same timeline, but there isn't shit we can do here."

As he walked toward the plane Roger assumed the agents and staff were following him. He pulled out his Manager and opened a text box for Miranda. She was logged back into GA+

Heading to your dad. We are uploading next week. Can you handle getting the family ready?

Roger stepped up the stairs and relaxed when he hit the cooler air-conditioned oasis on the plane. Before the revolution, a plane this size could transport 200 people; now it was a mobile office.

We are ready. Love you

13

Nick didn't say more than a few words the day before. That was fine with Kai. She spent the day on Sauce. She put the pill under her tongue the moment she was back in Nick's apartment. He was on the couch. Lying there in tears. She wasn't sure if he slept or ate, but either way, he was detached and unhappy. She knew it was her job to check on him and make sure he was OK, but she didn't have the time or space to deal with it. She resolved to talk to him later when she was not totally pizzled out.

The Sauce wasn't fully dissolved before she started feeling time expand. Words she was thinking seemed to float around her. There was a vague sense of a day passing, maybe a hundred years, it was hard to tell. While she was deep in the piz, she just let it ride.

When she woke up, it was done. Her sync was fixed, and her tech and biology were back on the same speed. She didn't look at the time, but she looked at the stats her Aver gained overnight. There were several dozen posts on social, and the items on her to-do list were moved to Done. Her house in the Sim needed a little more programming before she could live there, but most of her list of things to do was offline.

It said on her status that she prepared Foodle for Nick, but she didn't have the technology to give up her body and go phantom IRL.

Kai walked into the living room. Nick stood by the balcony looking west across the sprawl and the ocean in the distance. The sunlight was coming up behind them in the east, lighting the many towers of Santa Ana and Huntington Beach.

Kai saw the Foodle bottles in the sink, they were clean and ready for recycling. Someone had made them last night. The bookshelves were dusty. It seemed like Nick had not dusted or straightened them in years. She looked over to the life pod, which sparkled in the morning light. She didn't remember anything, except tripping balls. "Good morning."

He turned a little at the sound of her voice, and then back to the view. She walked up behind him, hoping to see what it was that was so amazing that he didn't even know she was there. Standing behind him, she saw it. His faded reflection in the glass and now hers. He raised his eyebrow as if he only saw her just now in the reflection. In ghostly form, in the window, Kai saw the Nick Mayerson she barely knew. She could tell there once was a younger, more handsome man in his place.

"Kai, may I tell you something?"

Kai smiled, "Sure, Nick."

"You are very beautiful, and I know, as an old man, how this sounds, but I very much enjoy your smile."

She laughed. "If you are going to flatter me, go on."

"An angel really." He turned and looked at her. It was uncomfortable, but he lifted his hand and rubbed the skin on her face. "It looks soft, the fresh skin of youth, but also augmented to absorb the UV."

Kai felt the air suck out of the room. Her smile faded; she knew the implication. Her first technological implant was given to her on the day of her birth. As she grew, she was modified and maintained. She had to work to pay for it all because living was almost impossible without them. There were jobs. Someone had to clean the Foodle tubes.

Before she was old enough to make a choice, her body was destined to be part machine. How could this old man, who was born natural and still granted basic human rights, understand what he was saying? How could he understand how offensive it was? She knocked his hand away.

"I didn't ask to be born this way, and when I had a choice, it was too late because this world is so fucked up by...well by you. Your generation."

Nick nodded. "Don't get angry at me. This might be all fake. "

"Or, it could all be very real. I am a human being, I have rights."

Nick laughed. "I am sure you feel that you do, but honestly, sweetheart, how do you know? As far as I know, you didn't exist before a week ago."

"I know what I am."

"Tell me about yesterday."

She pointed at him. "That's not fair."

"What? Asking you to remember yesterday?"

"I was pizzled, and I..." Nick let her words hang. She knew in her heart that the previous day was a blur. It just made her mad.

"You cleaned my apartment; we carried on a conversation."

"No, I didn't. Besides you didn't get up off the fucking couch."

Nick waved his hands. "Don't take this personally, Kai, I am not sure any of us are real."

Kai relaxed her stance a bit. He meant all of it. It was a reasonable question to have on your mind. The Sim she joined was not as advanced as the one he had been in. This could be part of the process that Nick needed to accept the idea of Heaven in his mind; to let go of his body. If so, then she knew she had to embrace this idea. She couldn't question it. Not now. She needed to get hi to upload and move on. It was best for him and for her as well. His family needed him. She would tell herself that to rationalize the whole thing. Kai took his hand into hers. His skin was older, but still soft. He did little with his hands while all she did was labor.

"Did you love her?"

"Who?"

"Your wife...Lisa, right?"

He nodded. "Bertrand Russell."

She looked confused for a moment. "I was talking about your wife."

"So am I. Her favorite Philosopher. Well, sometimes he was. I told you to read his work."

Kai nodded. She searched for the philosopher in her inner eye. "Epistemology."

Nick deepened his voice as if he were back at University for a lecture. "From Plato to Russell, all the way to this moment. You tell me, Kai, what is the distinction between the physical world and the mind?"

"That is a serious question to ponder before Coffee-ISH." Kai squinted and looked directly into his eyes. "Fuck Plato. I asked you about Lisa and you avoided the question."

"What question?"

"Did you love her?"

Nick looked at his bookshelves stacked three levels deep with philosophy textbooks and random biographies. "Nietzsche thought Kant was a moron."

"Love is a thing, right, as solid as this," She squeezed his hand. "Real enough that it reaches in and squeezes your heart. When that pod shut down and you were lying on the couch, a total sad sack, what were you missing?"

He nodded and whispered. "Her."

"Bertrand Rusell thought the distinction between the mind and physical world was total bullshit."

Nick grinned. "Not the metaphor he would've used."

"Nick, your body, my body, they will be gone one day. You of all people live up here." She tapped his forehead.

"It is a lie."

"Your truth is a truth."

She could see on his face he didn't like the sound of that. His grin faded as he spoke. "It was more than missing her. I looked around and had to ask myself the larger question."

"I think you are overthinking this."

Nick laughed and shook his head. "You never wondered if this was real? We have the technology to create a convincing reality. Maybe someone created this one, you don't know."

She could tell him that she knew, that she returned from GA+ glitching. It was impossible to take a hard stance on the reality of the natural world when it freezes like a buffering video and the words on the lips of the people around you look like a dubbed Turkish soap opera.

He released her hand and sat down on the couch. She felt a little despair. She wasn't changing his mind, and now he had her questioning herself. She looked out the window and back to Nick. The frustration must've been on her face. He sighed.

"I know you need me to upload, and I won't do it for you. I want to be with my family, and the idea that I will become just a thought scares the hell out of me."

She was about to say everyone becomes a thought, a memory, but Kai's Manager beeped. Her notifications lit up. The message was from Roger Greenstone. He was on his way here. She felt her stomach grip. She had failed to get Nick to agree to Heaven and now he was coming here. She felt the urge to beg but she knew it wouldn't do her any good.

"Hope you are ready for a visit."

"Who?"

"The White House sort of, well your son-in-law. I get the feeling he doesn't want to have this debate."

"Shit."

Kai had a feeling that Nick understood he was running out of time.

14

ROGER BLOCKED NOTIFICATIONS FROM the White House server. His staff were briefed that they were on a top-secret assignment. As they approached John Wayne airport just after the sun went down, the lights of Orange County and LA seemed to stretch into infinity. The far end of the landing strip was covered, and it was like landing in a tunnel. Water sprayed Air Force Four with coolant as the air brakes caught. He was handling personal business during the flight. He had received a confirmation from the church that would be performing the Uploading in Bethesda later in the week. The pastor, Barney Appleton, had worked out the details without involving the White House. It was a delicate balance, throwing around the weight of the White House, without alerting them.

As the plane rolled toward the airport Walter unlocked his belt. He had a skeptical look on his face. "I got the address for the church, and I am assigning a detail."

Walter Nelson was not a moron. The boss, as he liked the staff to call him, didn't want Roger and his family uploading until he solved the issue in Canada. Roger was not supposed to be making these arrangements, and he was on the far side of North America from the fallow fields in Canada. Walter always worked for the staff, never for the Boss himself, so Roger didn't know where his loyalties were.

"Thank you, Walter." Roger looked out the window and saw the electric Auto-Auto caravan waiting for them. He had to risk it. Walter hadn't objected yet. "Walter, you think we could handle this just you and I?"

Walter squinted a bit. "What's going on Mister Greenstone?"

Roger sighed. He waited until the rest of the staff headed for the front of the plane. "Let's talk in the Auto." They walked down the steps of the plane to the waiting Auto. The staff had loaded up in the other Autos to get to the hotel, having received their instructions from their Managers.

The electric SUV powered on as soon as they got in the back seats. "Auto protocol government level 5, disable all recording devices." Roger typed the address in his Manager and synced it to the Auto's operational control. They began to drive toward Nick's apartment.

"This is a personal matter. I know this is an abuse of my authority, but I can help your family too."

"How?" Walter shifted in his seat.

"Advice. Retirement. You up for the Heaven gold plan?"

"We were thinking about it. I need another year or so of service."

"Good," Roger shook his head. "Don't wait."

"I appreciate it sir, but I am in no rush."

Roger grinned. "Yes, you are. There is no fixing the situation up north. Foodle is going tits up."

"You're running?"

Roger shook his head. "No, I earned this retirement. Heaven is pretty much the only solution."

"The boss will have your brainbox flushed."

Roger nodded. "Yeah, he will. If he can find it."

"I see," Walter nodded. "I register your family's boxes under a bullshit name and you move up our dates."

"You'll need a few months to do the planning but if your family is augmented that should cut out some prep and get you in before stuff gets..."

Walter whistled. "That bad, huh?"

Roger nodded. Outside the window, they had already slid into the free-flowing traffic on the 405 going 85 miles per hour along the freeway. It was not as chaotic and filled with human error as the freeway system of his youth. Still, the swirling chaos to someone who lived most of his life in Sim was a little hard to take.

"Uploading is one thing," Walter looked out the window. "I'm not a greedy man Mister Greenstone."

"Come on Walter, I think at this point you can call me Roger."

Walter grinned. "Mister Greenstone, Encephalscans, Hubrizine treatments. I have two daughters. They are Augged, but it will still take some coin."

Roger used his Manager to tip Walter coins all the time. Little "thank yous" went a long way toward loyalty. Now he transferred 50,00 gold-plated Kibble. He saw the man lift an eyebrow.

"Down payment."

They circled the exit into the southwest side of Santa Ana and were stopped by traffic. Autos were stopped filling all four lanes coming off the freeway. The instant the Auto stopped the alert signaled to their Managers. Everyone knew that sound, the Lone Wolf alarm had a notorious tone, so no one had to take their Managers out of their pockets to know there was an active shooter.

A plugger drone floated outside their window and played an advertisement for NRA-sponsored real-time trackers. The pluggers and chasers were ad technology that the government approved after Roger had decided to spend most of his time in GA+, and they were disabled at the White House. He wanted to swat them away. There was an irony that it was bugging him now.

Walter unhooked his holster. Roger was not worried, as all White House detailed Autos were bulletproof. Roger leaned back in his seat and relaxed. He knew traffic wouldn't move for a while. He pulled up the local map, to see how far away the shooting was taking place. Walter was sharing his satellite link. It was tracking the shooter, and it could help them to get an idea of how soon they would be moving again.

The shooting was reported two blocks from the exit at a Foodle center. There was a red signal, which meant a civil disturbance of fifteen people are more. The national security feed Walter used actually listed the specific members of the crowd with voting rights. Only three of the twenty-seven gathered were citizens. He cringed at the information.

"This is gonna get ugly, Walter."

"We are trapped. Once the initial shooter is captured, we can move before the riot starts."

Some shooters just wanted attention, and many were bullied or grew up playing video games. Most were desensitized to the idea of shooting. This one seemed desperate. They were all desperate. Roger wondered why Walter was so sure a riot was coming.

"It is starting already," Walter whispered. He reached over to Roger's Manager and expanded the screen. The Foodle Center had closed hours early.

"You don't know that this is about Foodle...It could be isolated." Roger lied for a living. It was as easy as breathing. Intellectually, he understood that they were killing each other for the last scraps long before they landed in California, but in DC, he could think of these riots in abstract terms.

"He is coming this way, the shooter."

A man walked on the side of the road. His frame barely held up the dirty clothes on his body. He held out his Manger and it projected a hologram ad. *Will gig for Kib.* A Plugger ad drone floated behind the beggar advertising *Father Joe's unhoused person work program.* Roger didn't know why the man didn't click on the Plugger link.

"The shooter is almost here, Mister Greenstone," Walter said louder.

Roger looked down the street and saw the gunman. At this distance, it was clear, he had on a flak jacket, wore holsters on each leg, and he swerved around cars with his AR-15 lifted high. The shooter was running from a four-legged Robotacop that was coming down the sidewalk toward him like a mechanical cheetah. Two chaser-style Pluggers followed behind the gunman, projecting some kind of ad. Roger couldn't believe he was seeing chasers follow a lone wolf.

The gunman knew he was toast. Even at this distance, Roger could see it. Walter laughed. He must have seen it too. The Robotacop jumped and tackled the man. They heard him screaming. At first, it sounded like grunts, but he was saying something. One of the Robotacop's legs snapped the rifle like a twig, and the other snapped the gunman's wrist.

"Damn, that guy is lucky they can only disable," Walter snapped his holster shut.

Roger had made the Ad-runner Inc. deal while sitting on a beach in the Great American simulation. Pluggers were a technology that buzzed around looking to hop on your personal WIFI signal. That is how the ads target you. The Pluggers could project videos or holograms, but you could always walk away. The Chasers would follow, and if you didn't have the tip to make it stop it would make sure you saw that fucking ad. Ad-Runner's CEO Thurston Fernwright tipped a large amount of coin to make sure the approval happened in all branches of government. The lobbyists knew that the Congress and Senate were rubber stamps for the boss, but Kibble was a part of the system.

The Chasers kept following even as the gunman was being dragged further to the side by the Robotacop who was making sure traffic could flow. What ads were targeting this man? Roger was suddenly curious. The ads were meant to target your needs in real time, moment to moment. Curiosity got the best of Roger. He got out of the car. Moving in the evening heat of the hotbox was like walking tied to an anchor. The pavement still radiated incredible heat from the day's heavy sunlight. He faintly heard Walter protesting. The gunman screamed. "Where's the fucking Foodle? I just want to feed my fucking kids!"

Roger grabbed the first Chaser drone out of the air and pointed it so the video played on the sidewalk like a screen. The small drone responded in protest. "Ad interference is a $20 Kibble fine," it screamed before switching back to the ad. "Yucatan Almond paste for all your nutritional needs." Roger let go of the drone and grabbed the second one which was halfway through an ad for Blaze-Out, a fireman delivery service.

Walter came up behind him. "Mister Greenstone, traffic is opening up."

Roger looked down at the gunman struggling under the Robotacop. He should've felt sorry for him, but it was too late for that. They all made their choices. Here they were.

A crowd was gathered in the parking lot of the Foodle center. He could see them now. They were chanting. He couldn't tell what. A Plugger swung into his orbit. Roger grabbed it out of the air and pointed it towards the crowd. It read their servers and picked real-time ads.

Roger pointed the projector at the ground. The ad played for a series of items: stun guns, cutting tools, and a strange assortment of items. It was confusing.

"We need to go," Walter was angry and worried.

"No, shit." Roger walked quickly following him back to the Auto. Traffic had started to flow around them. Still, Roger was confused by the ads he saw and wondered why the Plugger was suggesting such strange items.

The Plugger in his path ID'ed him and spoke: *"Visting Orange County? Have you considered visiting the Disney Skypark?"*

Roger relaxed when he slid back into the air-conditioned comfort of the Auto. Walter snapped the door shut, and the Auto began to cross the streets toward Nick's building.

Roger couldn't be sure, but the combination of the stun gun and tools made grim suggestions to him. If there was no more Foodle, the next logical step for getting protein was one he didn't want to consider. He had to get this over with.

15

Kᴀɪ sᴇɴᴛ ᴛʜᴇ ᴛᴇxᴛ to her private chat with her Aver as she cleaned the counter in Nick's kitchen. The counter was clean, but she was trying to stay busy. The words flashed in the text box of her inner eye menu. She blinked the pattern to get control of her Ganglion and expand the text window. Three dots appeared. Her Aver was composing a reply. She looked back into the apartment, and Nick was out on the balcony looking at the lights and towers of Huntington Beach and the dark void of the ocean.

You need to build a network inside the Sim.

Kai read the words and wanted to scream. It was not her Avers's job. She put down the cleaning rag and pulled the Manager out of her pocket. Her fingers and thumbs moved like lightning across her tiny keyboard.

What does that even mean? I can build my network. Me. I can do that when I earn the coin to log in for real. You are Sim-sitting, squatting, and jacking signals to get in. If you get caught...

The reply came quickly.

> *Kai, slow down. Cut out the I business. I only exist as an extension of you. I am you. Everything that is you is me. I would never do anything you wouldn't do yourself.*

Of course, it would say that. The fact was Kai didn't post on all the socials like her Aver did. Insta, Friend-feed, Town-square, Neighborhub, or any of them. Her Aver posted there. Movie news, video tips, anger over Foodle prices, despair at the growing riots, conversations, light political opinions, and on so many platforms that she had wanted to engage in but lacked the time. Her Aver was posting on all of them, and everyone reading those words just assumed it was her.

It wasn't the first time, but in the back of her mind she wondered how many people she had interacted with over the years were even real. How many died and their Avers kept things going? Or how many were just letting their Avers socialize for them?

> *I don't even know what you have been saying. For all I know you have been telling the whole world crazy shit.*

Kai knew it wasn't true. The Aver was scary accurate. She couldn't count how many times she would see posts that predicted her responses perfectly. The one that scared her most was on Friend-feed.

A soon-to-be GA + neighbor posted it first, but it was all over her feed for the rest of the day.

> *Tell us the five bands you listened to in high school—don't lie.*

Kai's Aver posted with a response:

Led Zeppelin
Jimi Hendrix
Red Hot Chili Peppers
DJ Amelie
Greta Platt.

As Kai read 'her' answers on her Manger screen she felt a creeping dread. The honest response was generic AI-generated Aug-hop, but that would make her look totally basic. The answers she read were exactly what she would've answered. Sure, she listened to Zepp and Hendrix a bit because of her grandfather, but they were on the list for the same reason: retro cool-gal cred. The Chili Peppers was not as clear. It was true, all ninety-five albums were in her rotation, but many of those albums were AI-generated ones authorized by the estate of the band members. Those came out yearly now and were hardly "retro" as the punk-funk Aug-hop computer-generated era was now popular with young Simmys. DJ Ame was the Aug-hop pioneer whose music had never actually been heard by natural ears. Listing that artist counter-balanced the retro bands, making sure anyone reading the post would know that she was still a modern person. Greta Platt was a feminist icon and even though Kai was not much of a Platter she liked what mentioning her said about how independent she was. Men hated her, so there was a little bit of a middle finger having her on your list.

The list was bullshit, and exactly to the fucking letter what she would have answered. She felt her stomach drop. It was like having someone watching your thoughts; the smart and the stupid. It knew her better than she was willing to admit to herself. It was all there under the surface.

Her Aver responded:

Focus. Roger Greenstone is just minutes away. When he gets here. You need to look composed and helpful.

She hated that it was in her mind. Well, it wasn't, but it felt like it was right there in her head.

Why??? I failed. Nick is not close to uploading. I won't get the bonus. I needed that coin.

Kai looked at Nick looking thoughtfully outside. He was a good person. A deeply thoughtful man who missed his wife and wanted to spend time with his family. Kai couldn't understand why he was so attached to all this.

He is scared. He thinks he is dying soon. He believes this world is living... Comfort him.

"Shit," Kai whispered. "You're right."
Of course, I am. Frankly, I am sick of your shit.
This turn of events shouldn't have surprised her. Long before she had an Aver trained to be her online avatar, based on all her online content, she was pretty self-loathing. She hated herself and no one got madder at Kai than she did herself. She portrayed confidence, but it was an act. One that her Aver saw straight through. She felt another creeping feeling. Her Aver hated her. It lived half her life for her and...she didn't want to think about it.

Excuses. You were about to quit. You have a house and life waiting for you in the Sim. You'll be lying in a pod soon, while Friendlies sends some rook to clean your Foodle tubes.

Kai answered: *I don't know.*

The Aver's response was unexpected: *See it through. I'm out.*

Kai stopped and suppressed a scream. That fucking bitch, she thought as she realized the Aver was giving her a virtual cold shoulder. She stepped out into the living room. Her Manager signaled that Roger Greenstone's Auto was here.

"Nick, can we talk?"

"You still going to try and talk me into becoming compost?"

"Forget the money." She knew he didn't believe her. "I understand you are scared."

Nick grinned. "I don't trust Roger. Never did. My daughter, she loves him I suppose, but it always seemed calculated. A transaction. He doesn't care about my feelings. My fears."

Kai nodded. She was being careful. "You know I would switch places with you in a heartbeat, right?"

He laughed. "I can't trust you either. My truth is a truth. I don't follow your logic."

She laughed. No point in lying. "OK, you know I need the money. He is here, but I have to ask you Nick, are you willing to become nothing, to never see Miranda again?"

Nick looked out the window. "Kids today. You live on a series of signals, and you don't understand life. You have friends that are just names and a tiny picture. They exist in words in a feed of posts. They could be AI-generated ghosts. A second-generation copy of life, it means more to you than the real thing, so fuck living right? What is IRL but a hotbox and unending storms? It doesn't matter. Drinking protein paste? It doesn't matter. How many likes and reposts today? Lisa exists in that world, but it isn't her. Most humans that ever lived are lucky if they live on as memories."

Kai pointed at Nick's bookshelf. "Same as your philosophers. They live on as memories, right? We have always lived in those ways, as long as we have been making memories."

"Echoes at best. If you hear the echo of far-off music, is it the song you're hearing? The actual song or just echo?"

"A beautiful song or annoying one?"

Nick laughed. "For debate, a beautiful one."

She wanted to scream, "Just be a fucking echo!" But instead she said, "I still heard it. I experienced it."

There was a knock at the door. They looked at each other.

"You vote for his boss?"

Kai laughed at the question and shrugged. "What was the point?"

"Let the bastard in," Nick fell into his chair.

16

THE BUILDING WAS AIR-CONDITIONED, and thankfully, the Auto pulled into the garage below ground. Plenty of sticky humid air hung around them as they stepped out. A pair of Pluggers hovered by the door and came towards them. The machines read them as tourists and offered deals for on and offline parks. Walter unhooked his holster. The top floor of the garage was secured. The support classes didn't own as many vehicles, so many of the multi-level garages under the tower had been taken over by sunken villages. Many of them had self-sustaining economies and entire generations adapting to the conditions.

That was the reason Walter had his hand near his holster, but once they were in the lobby, he relaxed. The air conditioning roared like a plane engine. Still, the air was muggy. Roger wiped his forehead. A Plugger-style drone rose from behind the front desk.

"Visiting?"

"Nick Mayerson, he is in the apartment..."

"The elevator is waiting." There was a ding.

Walter nodded to let him know the building scan confirmed the path was secure.

The elevator brought hot air up with them, but once they got to Nick's level, forty floors above Santa Ana, most of the hot air had been filtered out.

The building was nice, and they had paid a pretty penny to move his Father-in-Law higher above the hotbox. In the years following Lisa's death, the battle to get him to move above the heat dome was the first fight they had.

Nick said he didn't want to leave his home, but once the dark evenings failed to cool the air, he relented. You can argue ideas until you are blue in the face, but temperature and storms have a way of ending climate change debates.

At Nick's door, he paused and gave Walter a look. They worked together long enough that he didn't need to ask Walter. He was planning on keeping guard outside. He just nodded.

Roger lifted his hand to knock, and the door recognized him. A video screen built into the door lit up. The video was an AI-generated image of Paula Key, the Insta-influencer who became famous for her two-minute ab-tightening yoga videos.

"Hello [Roger], thanks for visiting Santa Ana towers. Would you like to order a gift for your host?" Paula made a kissy face and wagged her finger. "Don't be rude."

Roger blinked three times to close the ad and rapped the door with his knuckle on her fading face.

There was a slight delay before the door opened. His Janie Kai answered the door. He remembered her from the video chat. Her bright blue eyes were more striking in person. Her wild, multi-colored hair pulled attention off the rest of her. She tried her best to hide it with make-up, wild hair, and clothes, but Roger knew instantly that she was at least 50-P. It didn't matter anymore, but he had a habit of looking for signs of a person's voting status. He didn't get where he was by being nice to people he didn't need to.

"Ahh the help. Well, ideally the *help*."

He liked the benefits of his status. He enjoyed swinging his dick around in Canada. He hated that he couldn't force the asshole to fix his problems. He had to depend on Walter. It felt good to have a little of the power dynamic back over this young woman.

He could tell she was reading Convaid suggestions. If her program was well-trained, it would suggest three methods of kissing his ass. She said nothing and just smiled, so he knew he was right. Kai wanted badly to tell him off, but not after she had failed at her very simple mission.

"Is something wrong my dear?" Roger smiled, knowing she was seething.

"Don't be rude, Roger. She did your bidding." Nicked rocked in his chair.

Kai closed the door behind him. Roger took off his suit jacket and held it out waiting for Kai to take it. She just walked past him.

"Does that mean you will be heading back with me to DC?"

"I didn't think there was a rush. According to you we have eternity."

Roger pointed at Kai. "Do you mind?"

Kai was confused. "Mind what?"

"I would like to have a private conversation with my father-in-law."

Kai looked at Nick. "I don't care whose Kibble is in my account, I work for Nick."

Nick smiled, "It's fine, sweetheart, I appreciate it."

Kai didn't look at Roger at all. "I'll be in the bedroom if you need me."

They watched her leave the room. Roger walked over to the overcrowded bookshelves, which were three levels deep. Nick had spent decades collecting them. Hardly anyone reads books anymore. No one would buy them. They would be in flames in a few weeks. Roger hated these books.

"She tried Roger. Don't blame her, it is me. I think I want to die the old-fashioned way. I will talk to Miranda and explain my position."

Roger wagged his finger. "She loves you more than me. Almost as much as the kids. She won't upload without you. Can you please just think about her?"

"She should respect my desires; I am sure they can generate a reasonable version of me."

Roger groaned so deeply he worried it might sound comical. He grabbed a chair from the dining room table flipped it around and sat closer to Nick than he ever had.

"I have suggested that a dozen times. Your daughter thinks you are such a unique snowflake that no computer can fake you."

"That seems dramatic."

"You convinced her," Roger pointed at the bookshelf.

Nick knew exactly what he was saying. Roger could see it dawning on him. '*No fake Lisa could be replaced by the books on the shelf that contained her wisdom and experience.*' Roger was in this mess because of that collection.

"I see," Nick whispered.

"I don't understand why you won't do this for her?"

Nick didn't answer right away. "Professional hazard, I spent my whole life asking the big questions. I hated the feeling of being out of my body. I don't think I am because I think. I think I am because I feel." Nick squeezed his finger. "I want to die like a human being, not a brain floating in gunk."

It was time to play hardball. Roger was going to have to disarm Nick a little. This man never personally saw what kind of asshole he was capable of being.

"I know what you mean to my wife, but can I be honest with you?"

Nick weighed his response. "I might regret this, but sure, be honest."

"I don't give one literal shit about you. I have throughout my whole career made life-and-death decisions that have killed children, put families on the street, and lined the Boss's pocket. One of the few people I care about is your daughter and grandchildren. They want you to be with us. So will you trust me when I say that I am telling you a nasty secret that, you can believe me, is absolutely true?"

Nick nodded.

"Great. I would be fine fooling the family with a generated Nick. In fact, we could make him less full of himself. But, I need you there for the process, so at least Miranda believes you are joining us. You jump through the hoops and convince her for me, then you can come back here and die alone."

Nick thought about it. Roger didn't care what choice he made, but he knew it would be better if he was really on board.

"Just one more thing," Roger added. "It is not public yet, but if you have been following the shooter forecast and the growing number of riots, you can see it coming."

"See what coming?"

"The Foodle is running short."

"By how much?"

Roger nodded. "By enough. Things are going to be changing quickly."

Nick closed his eyes. "Bastard."

"Sticks and stones, Nick. What's done is done. We had a good time. We fulfilled every promise the Boss made."

"You can't be serious."

"We did more than make America great again, we made it perfect. Better than that, we offer you Heaven. Literally, eternal bliss. Promises kept, if you...think about it."

"Pay up or starve to death."

"That is an awfully negative way to see it." Roger stood up and pushed the chair with his foot to the table. "Besides, I'm paying for your spot, asshole. So pack your bags. We leave in twenty minutes."

17

Melissa read the weather report on her Smart-Gogs. Dust-off, big one. Since she stole the mountain bike and left Berkeley, she rarely took them off. Life in the Bay Area was becoming too expensive, and Janie work was not even close to paying the bills. Violence among the support class was on the rise. It was frustrating, sleeping beauties in the pods always got fed. Without the Simmers' blissful ignorance of how bad the world had gotten, there would be no income for people like her. Most Janies had to cut ten or fifteen percent of the Foodle powder in each serving just to have enough for themselves.

She was able to take her bike on the Hyperloop train as far as Santa Barbara. For a time, things looked better. She spent a few months there, cleaning the tubes of a woman who hosted a talk show in GA+. She was just getting comfortable in the house when they fired her. Celebrities could be paranoid.

Melissa heard rumors about mountain towns that were higher up where the temperature was more reasonable. Crops grew, and the water was plentiful. One of the growing freedom zones, off the books. Once she got to Ventura, she headed east on a trail for bikes. She was ten miles inland when she read about the dust-off, and she hit the wall of sand. A high-pressure system had been sitting on the Mojave Desert for the last week like a house guest who wouldn't leave. The forest that had buffered the small California mountain town of Ojai for centuries had died decades earlier. The exodus of celebrities and their money had been quick, and the little town suffered.

The dust-off was only going to last a few hours, according to the weather report floating in her goggles. She pulled over, wrapped up in a blanket, and waited. She fell asleep in her makeshift cocoon and woke with an hour of storm to go.

Her connection with a server was dodgy, not strong enough for gameplay but she read her socials. The storm slowly died as she scrolled through growing posts complaining about Foodle prices, riots, and President Supreme. She knew those accounts would get suspended quickly. Most people posted videos and text in metaphors. She couldn't remember seeing this much frustration.

When the roar of the desert wind finally stopped, she stood and shook off her blanket. Her Gogs were so dust-covered she couldn't see anything, except the computerized text. She took them off and shook them out.

The sand covered the town like a brown, gritty version of a white Christmas. Not that she knew what snow looked like outside of old movies. Melissa shook out her blanket and cleaned and oiled her bike chain. A calm quiet came over the central California town. Melissa didn't like the stillness.

The rumors were bullshit. The hotbox was just as bad here as anywhere. Now that the sun wasn't fighting a sandstorm anymore, Melissa felt like she was suddenly standing in a frying pan. Her cooling tats and subdermal ice worked to cool her body. Her internal Augs were flashing a warning in her inner eye: *Get to shade.*

She needed to make it to a city like Los Angeles, where she could climb up out of the hotbox. This dirtside shit was not going to work. The monitor in her Gogs was flashing several warnings about her temps. Melissa had a love-hate relationship with her Augs, but they were trying to keep her alive right now.

Under her goggles were entirely mechanical eyes that gave away her status as 50-P. Her actual number rounded up to 65-P for legal purposes. She had been able to vote when she was younger and even kept her citizenship for two years after that before a tax audit outed her to the city of Berkeley. After thirty-two years of hating it, she kind of missed her hometown.

Melissa wondered where the people were. She walked her bike slowly, looking for any sign of life. Empty stores, gas stations, and lots of silence. In the distance, she could just barely make out the post office in the shape of a tower. A sign that read "WELCOME TO OJAI," hung by one nail and danced in the light breeze. The nail squeaked as the sign tapped the post, and it was the only sound she could hear. When the automatic door from a grocery store opened, Melissa jumped.

A softball-sized Plugger floated outside and moved toward her. Who knows when the last time this ad drone had a customer? She didn't want to pay to skip the ad, so she braced to be sold a product like goggle cleaners, or bike parts, or something it thought she needed.

She didn't stop for the Plugger so it had to speed up to catch up to her. It got in her path and played the ad straight to her goggles.

The video glitched a bit, it said her name funny, but it took up her vision. *"Hey Mel, welcome to Ojai California. Were you looking for weapons? You might want to consider a Glock 9mm. Perfect for holding off roving bands of attackers."*

Words flashed in red on her goggle lens: *Guaranteed delivery in just fifteen-minutes for Gold-level members.*

Melissa stopped and looked around. Delivery from where? She waved the Plugger away.

The heat rose quickly now. She had enough technology to balance it for a while, but her server was flashing warnings for all of her biological and technology systems. The grocery store was going to have to do until nightfall.

As she walked to the door the Plugger came back. It stayed at a distance so she couldn't swipe it.

A second video came on of a man with a long beard, dirty teeth, and a camouflage hat. "Cleaning kits for hunting! This is basic survival gear everyone in the central coast needs..."

Large mammals were extinct in the region. They were down to rabbits, and she didn't like what that ad may have meant. Melissa shut down the ad.

She would live with the loss of coin to turn it off. She would also just have to brave the heat to get the fuck out of this town.

When she mounted the bike she heard the explosion. It sounded like thunder but she knew it was a rifle. It kicked the dirt beside her.

Melissa's heart raced and she pedaled so hard her legs burned. She had a few blocks to get back to the bike trail. She didn't look back to see what kind of car or truck might be following her, but she heard it roar to life, and it was getting closer.

Melissa braced for the car to hit her from behind. The entrance to the bike path was just ahead. If she could make it the entry was too narrow for a vehicle to follow. She never saw the rope as it pulled tight and hit her at chest level. She bounced on the pavement and hit her head. Melissa gained consciousness for a few seconds, enough to hear the laughter of her captors.

———

SeeJay didn't sit in the public observation lounge often. It was crowded, and the gravity was heavier in the room. So, he sat one floor lower with a lighter gravity setting and a smaller window. The earth took up the whole view from here. Some people felt it was easier in this room to forget you were in orbit. The other residents on the Vikram Sarabhai space station often stopped what they were doing when they passed this window on their way home to enjoy the view. SeeJay didn't miss India, but he did miss his cats and bass guitar he left in Bangalore.

He set his Manager up on the window and since they were crossing over Britain, he played Black Sabbath. They were his favorite band, so he hardly needed the excuse. *Into the Void* would be the most fitting song, but the rumbling rhythm of *Children of the Grave* is what echoed through the space station instead.

Britain looked so dark compared to the first time he saw it from the shuttle window that brought him here. The very lights of civilization were disappearing everywhere.

This was his depression ritual. The crop failed again. Zero G was not any better for growing food than the gardens in the raised cities above India. The logic was that if they could control the environment, they could feed the country. This season would be the third wave of die-offs.

SeeJay wasn't a fan of the decision, but there was little they could do. The team on the station could grow enough food to stay alive and as long as they kept the station rotating and spent enough time in gravity daily, they would survive. They were the lucky ones. The ravages of life in orbit were tough on the body, but they could manage.

Ozzy's voice echoed in the space station. Geezer Butler wrote those lyrics, and he thought things were pretty bad at the time. As a bass player, SeeJay thought about Geezer a lot. He wished he were a part of that generation that could grow old and die.

SeeJay loved playing bass. The low end was his favorite part of heavy metal music. It appealed to him almost as much as the purr of his cats. He was always good at math, and ended up a scientist, in orbit, trying to monitor the oxygen production of plants.

He noticed condensation was obscuring his view of the Earth. There was nothing comparable to seeing everything from orbit. It changes people. Far too few people have that experience. You can try to explain to people that they are living on an incredibly fragile, tiny island in the vast cosmos, but they don't get it.

SeeJay would rather think about Sabbath..

With his index finger, he touched the window and wrote out a message in the condensation: RIP. It could've been for Earth or for Geezer. Maybe both.

⸻

Melissa tried to wake herself up. She knew she was inside a bag. Humidity and the smell of her own fear were suffocating. They had ripped her Gogs off, but her Inner Eye menu kept working. Using her Ganglion, she accessed her menu, and even as she was knocked out, her Augs were collecting information. Three people were holding her hostage. Her Ear-pal recorded their voices. There were two men who answered to "Bobby" and "Austin", and a woman hey called "Daisy."

Melissa was lucky she was still getting a signal. She pulled up a map and saw that she had traveled four miles from her bike. According to her tracker, her wheels were still back in town, and the electric motor was still at 12%. That information didn't help her. She was higher in the hills now. This had been a national forest before the Second Revolution. According to the map they were at McFeffe's Christmas tree farm. At least, it had been the last time the address was registered more than a decade ago.

The Auto stopped and she heard a faint wind outside. Melissa suppressed a scream. Her Aver sent her a message.

I am looking for an escape, but they are armed.

No shit.

The bag zipped open. Daisy was a pale-skinned and lightly freckled white lady with dirty blonde hair and teeth that had seen better days. She put her finger over her lips. Melissa was just glad to breathe some fresh air.

Daisy tied her hands together before lifting her out. She had practice. She had done this many times. Daisy was a Nat, or if she had any Augments they were minor. She was sweating buckets. Internal moisture recyclers were an operation most got as toddlers. Even people with barely any auguments had those.

Melissa scanned the area. High desert, dead stumps, and sad attempts to grow trees that failed years ago. A large pile of bones made afire pit that looked big enough to grill a bear in.

The two men were setting up tools in an open-air shed. Melissa felt a wave of nausea and had trouble standing. She fell to her knees and Daisy tried to lift her.

"You're cannibals."

"Shut up," Daisy grunted as she got Melissa to her feet.

Her Aver spoke softly inside her head:

Step behind her, You are just tall enough to put your rope over her head. With your augmented strength you can choke her out in five seconds.

Melissa sent a text back: *The guys will shoot me.*

Her Aver answered:

Use her as a shield and die fighting. Better yet, live.

"This ain't right, Daisy," Melissa whispered.

"How do you know my name? Never mind. Shut up." She pushed Melissa harder.

"I just want to get back to my bike. I didn't see a thing. I won't tell anyone."

Daisy stopped and looked at her. "We ain't doing nothing wrong."

Melissa could see in the woman's eyes she believed this. "You're eating people!"

Daisy shook her head. "You ain't no person. You're a computer that carries around a little meat. You take care of people, real people, but you ain't people. Not really."

It wasn't the first time she heard anyone talk like this. It was part of life when you were 50-P. She had been arguing for her rights since she was a child, but never in a situation like this. She heard of Nats who thought they were the only children of God.

"We were starving, drinking that bullshit." The bigger of the two men whom Melissa assumed was Austin walked closer. "We would never eat a person. A real person created by God."

"I was born. I had a mom and dad, just like you."

Austin leaned in closer, he was so close that Melissa could smell his rotten breath. "Those ain't eyes. God didn't give you those. The flesh you have is an insult, being carried around by a computer. Wasting air for God's creatures. I won't starve for you, abominations."

Strangle him now. Her Aver shouted in her head. Melissa screamed and swung her roped hands over Austin's thick neck. She needed the augmented strength for work as she often had to lift clients out of their life pods, and some of them were overweight. She rarely used it but now she was grateful for it.

Austin's throat collapsed quickly. She spun around in time to let his body absorb the shotgun blasts that Bobby fired at her. Austin's body shook under the impact. A few of the shotgun pellets went straight through him and blasted into Melissa.

She collapsed, twisting Austin's body to the side. "Fucker!"

Bobby stood over her before he saw the pistol she had pulled out of Austin's leg holster.

"Shit," were his last words before Melissa fired. He fell backward. Melissa felt a certain level of relief, but the pain in her chest was already setting in.

So sorry, Melissa. That didn't work as planned.

Don't be. We were already dead. You did your best.

Melissa didn't want her Aver feeling bad, but fear was setting in. She activated her death protocols. Her Aver would automatically inform all her socials that she was gone and continued to make Happy Birthday posts for her top 30 social connections every year, and donate her kibble to family and friends.

Melissa bled quickly; it wouldn't take long now. She used all of her strength to sit up. Daisy stood above her holding a knife. Now Melissa was able to get a better look at the woman. She was in her twenties, at best. She had probably never left these hills. In some ways, Melissa couldn't blame her. The

Generations before were the ones to blame for the way everything had turned out. They had it all and didn't care about the world they were leaving to those of us not yet born.

Melissa was glad she got two of them. She wondered if Daisy would end up eating her. She wouldn't eat Austin and Bobby. They were people to her.

Before Melissa closed her eyes, she thought she saw Daisy lick her lips.

18

Kai slapped a listening dot on the wall before returning to the bedroom. If the Secret Service agent hadn't been waiting outside, she wouldn't have risked it. But it was her job on the line, so she decided it was worth it. She followed every word of the argument that Nick had with Roger Greenstone on her Ear-pal. She knew Roger's voice from the news, and he wasn't kind the first time they talked, but the White House Chief of Staff was a bigger asshole in person than she ever imagined. The back and forth was predictable, but one thing got her attention. When he said the Foodle was running out, her whole body tensed up. It wasn't like she didn't suspect that was already happening, but you wouldn't know it from watching the news or reading socials. Negative posts got buried by the administration filters, and the news was sponsored by the State.

The first clues about the Foodle situation spread two ways: word of mouth and the NRA-sponsored Lone-wolf alerts. Everyone knew that shootings were on the rise, but it was the twenty-first century and gun violence had been the American way since before Kai was born. Bad news had always driven more gun sales. But, the riots over Foodle were a new thing.

The optimists thought it was only a blip; a bad growing season. Older folks remembered when President Supreme saved them from the liberals who hurt the farmers with their over-regulation. She was young, but she remembered the God Bless Foodle ad campaign that played on the early Plugger drones.

Twenty-minutes. Greenstone had said that in twenty minutes he was taking Nick with him. She wasn't even sure she would be allowed to stay the night here. She would have to get back home to the city. She would have to find out what the train schedules were.

Kai looked at her stuff spread out across the room. She hated packing. She opened her Manager, and she had notifications from Friend-feed. Six included violation notices from the Friend-Feed admin warning her that if she posted another community violation, she would get a week's suspension. This was strange. She didn't post risky stuff. What was her Aver doing?

Code A: Unpleasant post violation. Code F: Fake story.

Kai was curious now. The article wouldn't be available, but she would be able to see the thumbnail and headline in the violation report.

"Berkeley Janie killed by Cannibals in Ojai Valley." This story is unverified and deemed fake news by the Ministry of Truth.

Kai messaged her Aver: *Why did you share a post that was a violation?*
Her Friend-feed was filled with pictures of this woman, and her name was trending. Hashtags and Ganglion hooks for inner eye menus sent everyone to her picture. The one most people were sharing was a selfie she took just before her Aver instituted her death plan.

Melissa Childan. Say her name. Don't forget Melissa and what happened to her.

Her Aver wasn't answering. It was still mad at her. A knock on the door pulled her attention away.
"Come in."
Nick opened the door and stood in the doorway. "Kai, we need to talk."
"You gotta go. I am happy for you."

"Did you listen? Be honest because we don't have lots of time."

Kai didn't have the time to feel caught. She nodded.

"I need to go." Nick didn't sound happy. "And I think I am going to do the bullshit."

Kai nodded and gave Nick a grin. "I'll pack up. I liked arguing with you."

"Yes, but Kai, I want you to come with us."

"I've never left LA. Well California. You know what I mean." When Kai said it she sounded pathetic. She had traveled and had seen other places inside Sims. A part of her was scared to go so far away. A text popped up from her Aver.

They ate her. Melissa Childan. Her Aver got the word out before the ministry shut it down.

"Sweetheart, the Foodle is running out."

Nick assumed it was his words that broke her. It was all of it. She struggled to speak at first. "I don't have the money to upload."

Nick pointed at her. "DC will have food longer. Give yourself a chance. I've told Roger I won't go without your support. If you are at the upload...well, I can get around your legal status."

It meant so much to Kai. She was shocked he cared. Her own mother didn't care about her that way. Mom? Kai felt guilty at the idea of leaving and never seeing her again.

We have to go. The West Coast is a tinderbox.

She didn't need convincing from her AI.

Kai held up her Manager for Nick. "It is already starting, isn't it?"

Nick looked at the banned headline. "Can you leave in ten?"

Kai nodded. After he closed the door, she opened a video chat and waited until her mother's face filled her screen. Her mother was in a typical, wealthy Hollywood home. She could see the sprawl of LA lights behind her. Carrie Dame was still a Janie, supporting many wealthy families on the same block in Beverly Hills was her full-time job. She stayed under the poverty line just enough to earn a yearly Sim vacation.

"Hey Mom, why are you still at work?"

"I am waiting for a Foodle delivery. Doctor Rittersdorf is Simmed, but her Foodle is really overdue."

Kai closed her eyes and braced herself. She knew how this was going to go. "Mom, I'm not sure it is coming."

"Oh, don't start with that fake news cry-baby shit. The lib-tards and communists are doing this. They think everyone has a right to Foodle, even drug addicts."

"Mom, please, just listen."

"Honey, you didn't read my e-mail, did you?"

Kai scrolled through five messages from her mother. Most of the others were President Supreme-sponsored ads for Heaven-Gold. So, she ignored them.

"You are not the only one moving to Great America Plus! I finally did it!"

The great upload. The ruling class were probably getting warnings now, and they were running. That explained why the space on the server was freeing up, but the question remained who would work and support us? GA Plus needed a healthy body to operate. If there was no Foodle or Janies to support them, there was no point in logging on.

"Mom, think about it. Why is so much bandwidth opening up?"

"The Promise of Great America, baby. We made it. You and me both."

Kai held up a finger. "The riots, the increased shooters. Mom, how late is that Foodle delivery?"

"What are you trying to say, Kai?"

"I think we're fucked, the whole thing. America. Great America. It is all dying."

A look of anger came over her mother's face. "How dare you! After everything the President sacrificed for us. Don't be a traitor, baby, he can fix it. He always does. You gotta have faith."

"Mom, I am going with my client to DC, and I am not coming back. I am going to try to upload to Heaven. You should too."

"I don't have that kinda money, but when we live in Sim we can..."

"Just find a way, and Mom, no matter what happens..." Her mom always frustrated her. But she was the first face she saw, and the last voice she heard at night as a child for so many years. "I love you, please stay safe."

Kai canceled the call and let out her breath. Her bag was packed. It was amazing how quickly the world could end. In a matter of minutes, the life she knew was over.

19

Kai was just leaving the guest bedroom when the Secret Service agent stepped in her way. He blipped her with his ID: **Walter Nelson—Secret Service**.

"Normally, there is a security clearance before getting on Air Force Four."

"We are on four?" Nick laughed. "I thought we were more important than that. Air Force Two at least?"

Nelson didn't seem like the joking type, at least not when they were two minutes from leaving. "I came to get your consent to an automatic shut-down protocol. If you don't try anything dangerous, it won't matter." Shutdown orders would null out her augments. They didn't need her consent. He was being polite.

It was a scary prospect; the idea that they could snap your eyes off, but that was the cost of having such powerful technology behind your eyelids.

Kai looked him over and asked, "Do *you* give consent?"

"It is standard policy for government service 50-P officers."

"Agent Nelson, you are more machine than I am." Kai pointed at Roger across the apartment. "And given Mister Greenstone's age..."

Walter shook his head. "I would not bring that up."

"Hypocrisy is a sensitive topic, got it." Kai grinned, "Mister Mayerson is the only voter on the plane."

"You'll find, in DC, legal exceptions are a way of life."

Nick held his small duffle bag and watched them from the door.

"Yeah, whatever." Kai grabbed her bag and walked past him. Nick held open the door and smiled as they filed out. He took one last look around. He walked over to the bookshelf. Kai used her zoom lens to read the title on a book Nick picked up. *The Debate Over Reality* by Lisa Harris Mayerson. Nick held the spine under his nose, smelled the book, and then held it to his heart.

"It was her personal copy. She always took it with her to teach from."

"Nick, we have to go," Roger said without a hint of patience.

"Bring it with you," Kai said. "Keep it."

Nick ran his finger across all the books, then he was ready to go.

* * *

There were more staff than Kai ever expected on the plane. They were all talking and working on various aspects of government business and didn't seem to notice the old man and his Janie boarding the plane.

She didn't count, but there seemed to be at least a dozen staff traveling with them. A couple of them were Secret Service agents. There was an office up front and twenty seats in the back. Roger went straight up to the office and never once asked them if they wanted to go up front. Kai assumed they were not invited, and Nick didn't seem interested.

She and Nick had a row to themselves in the back, near the bathroom. Nick held his wife's book across his chest. They had waited most of the night at the airport, while flight plans were filed, and the staff arrived. Kai was both happy to finally be on the plane and filled with terror at facing this new experience.

The staff gave them a few curious looks, but they could get Nick's ident-files from a quick search. They didn't wonder about her once they had his name.

Kai had never been in a real plane, but she had flown inside Sims a couple of times. They were flying toward dawn and a part of her was excited to see the country. She looked out the window and connected all her servers to the ones they allowed on the plane.

"Do they even have pilots anymore?" Nick asked. Kai shrugged and then tapped the shoulder of a person sitting in front of them. This man was already Simmed out and didn't respond. There was a woman two rows ahead who was lifting a suitcase into a carry-on bin.

"Excuse me, do you know if there is a pilot on the plane?"

She shook her head. "The best pilots work from home in the Sim."

Kai believed it, but she could see it bothered Nick. He shook his head. "I would like to relax on the flight."

"You are fine, it is Air Force Four."

That didn't assure Nick. The woman with the suitcase walked toward them. "You're Roger's father-in-law?"

Nick put up his hands. "Guilty as charged."

She laughed. "Miranda is a good friend. We vacation in Italy together."

Nick's eyes narrowed. "Right, Kayleigh Miller. That was a few years back, right?"

"Two summers ago."

"Interesting..." Nick wagged his finger at her and grinned.

Kai noticed something seemed to be bothering the woman. She gave him a polite smile and returned to her seat. Nick looked at Kai. "Sim-cation. I saw the moments reel. It looked beautiful."

"Why was she offended by your shit-eating-grin?"

"I didn't recognize her because two summers ago, she looked thirty years younger in the Sim."

"So?"

"I just found it interesting. I think she was offended because I reacted."

Kai shook her head. "That is old people shit. You folks worry about the differences my generation doesn't. How you present in the Sim has fuck all to do with the real world."

"She is my generation," said Nick.

"Right, who cares?" Kai clicked her seatbelt on. "She can be who or what she wants in the Sim."

Nick raised an eyebrow and got comfortable in his seat as the plane rolled out.

Kai set Friend-Feed to auto-scroll and commented on a few posts to pass the time, hoping to zone out during takeoff. The roar of the plane was impossible to ignore. She looked around. Half the staff were in a simulation already, the rest were working or doing something, and no one seemed to notice the take-off but her.

She gripped the seat as the plane soared into the air. The heat pressure dragged the plane a bit.. She relaxed when they were finally airborne. A few minutes later, they climbed higher than the clouds.

Kai leaned her forehead against the window. They turned out over the mountains, and for a brief moment, she saw the morning sun hitting the towers all across the Los Angeles region. LA was her real world. The only other experience she had was online.

The unending sprawl left nothing of nature. Life in the towers was something she always knew growing up. It never seemed strange to her. Nature was a thing she only experienced when it was designed to be experienced.

The plane turned. Mountains and deserts; real nature rolled under her. In the corner of her vision, the messages and posts kept scrolling. The normal stuff she would see: *Citizen Savior* stats, Kibble counts, Foodle combos to help with flavor, and work-outs were sprinkled in her feed, but it was a strange morning. The Janie killed up north was a story that wouldn't die. Melissa Childan's Aver seemed to be fooling the system. It was creating new profiles and posting her last video everywhere. When it would get censored, the Aver created new accounts and kept posting. The rumors were that the video was disturbing, but you couldn't look away. Kai dreaded seeing it, but every time the censors crashed the video she wanted to see it more.

Every time Kai would open the video it would buffer for a few seconds and a warning would pop up and tell her that this content was not available. She gave up and looked out the window, closing the feed. She just wanted to see the country. So far, all she saw was sand.

"What are you gonna do, Roger?" The President was red-faced and angry. He had unplugged from the Sim and woke up his mostly robotic body to jump on this video call. His lead staff all cringed.

Roger pulled his chair up to the table. He was still on Air Force Four. He put his Manager down and wondered how he should tell the boss he didn't have a clue what he was so livid about. He decided to respond about Canada, as that was most likely.

"Sir, you will not like this, but the situation in Canada is more than just dire. The crops are failing for a third season and there..."

"Canada?" The President leaned closer to his camera. They were almost looking up his nose. "Who said a damn thing about Canada?"

Roger's staff looked at each other in panic. They were all thinking the same thing. He didn't explain himself, and they were expected to know what he was upset about.

Roger had played this game since the President was a full slob held together by diet Coke and cheeseburgers; now he was a brain with a frighteningly low IQ floating in a vat of Hubrizine, inside a skull meant to look like the head he was born with. His robotic body was just the latest means to keep him from having to give up the presidency—the greatest ego boost in the life of someone trying to undo the psychological damage done by his judgmental father.

He knew this game, and no one played it better than Roger. "Mister President, I'm sorry we are not as well informed as you are. Could you get us up to speed?"

He leaned back and nodded. "The video of the loser on the west coast. Come on, the dumb bitch that got herself killed. You know the one."

Alex, one of his longest-running staff and a 70-P Master of Technology, quickly forwarded a video to Roger's inner-eye menu. Roger used his Ganglion to expand the video to fifty percent of his vision and let it play.

The video was shot by drone. Thankfully the lighting was not ideal. It was still hard to look at. A woman hung by her tied hands in what looked like a barn. It was impossible to deny the suffering of this woman, but Roger got a sinking feeling when he saw her right eyelid was closed. The drone shooting the video was her augmented right eye that took flight to film her. That implied a desperation to create a last plea for help.

"Oh great, my Chief of Staff is just seeing it now. Great. They are saying, 'Sir, how can this happen, sir?' They are asking me, and you don't even know."

The woman in the video was bleeding in her midsection. She was crying and sobbing in pain. Roger didn't feel anything for this woman, but something about this video had upset the boss and it was his job to keep what remained of the President happy and functioning.

Who is this woman? Roger sent a text to Alex who was sitting next to him.

"Her name is Melissa Childan," he whispered. "She is a support class worker who grew up in Berkeley. Her last registration had her working in Santa Barbara."

The President heard him. "She is making a mess, Roger. Big mess, ugly mess. Huge."

Roger watched the video and couldn't believe she was still alive. Then he heard her voice. "My name is Melissa Childan and if you are seeing this video, I'm already dead. A victim of a dying system. I was attacked in Ojai, California by a group of desperate people. There is no Foodle reaching these hills, and the people...they are going to eat me. Cannibals. But, I don't blame them..."

Roger shut down the video and wanted to scream. He needed one more week, but now the President would understand how fucked they were. Despite all their efforts, the video of this woman was being seen everywhere. This was about Canada, but the boss was too much of an idiot to see it.

"You see, Roger? You see what a fucking mess we have now."

He did, and he had no answers. No solutions anymore. Roger looked across the office. The plane hit a little turbulence, and the President's video glitched a little. Walter Nelson shrugged at him. Roger had no choice but to lie.

"Sir, there is no reason for you to worry. Go back home." By that, Roger meant his simulated estate in Great America Plus which was modelled after his golf course in Florida. "We are working on some actions, including emergency Foodle to the danger zones."

"A wife saw this, Roger. She said to me, you know what she said, Roger? What are you gonna do honey?"

"I understand, Mister President."

"She didn't say what is Roger going to do, she asked me."

"We're on it, Mister President."

"It is all over Great America, the people are talking Roger. Not good Roger. When the people ask and they say, they say, 'Sir, will the Foodle show up?' I tell them, yes. They've got to show up, Roger."

Roger nodded, "You tell the first ladies we are working on a solution."

No goodbye. The President clicked the video off. All the staff looked at Roger. Alex leaned closer and whispered. "What solution?"

Roger shook his head at Alex. "Get your affairs in order, my friend."

A natural human eye looking out a window at America as it passed under them would see very little. Autos that looked like ants, fields, and fields of green. Kai saw nothing but flat brown dirt. She had used the zoom in her advanced eye to get a better look earlier. New Mexico was devoid of activity, and in Texas, she saw little movement except in Dallas and Fort Worth. Those cities didn't look that different from LA, built to the sky. The tower's platforms were clear to see from her side of the plane. They passed five miles to the south of the Dallas city line. It was the only life she had seen so far on the flight.

Nick stirred in the seat next to her. She stood and slid past him in the aisle. Kayleigh Miller was in her seat, looking at her Manager's screen. It was a tough angle, but Kai saw what she was watching, and she held in a gasp. Beaten and hanging, Melissa Childan begged for her life. Kayleigh Miller closed the video and stood up. She looked down the aisle, feeling caught, seen. Kai smiled at her. Nick thought she was a similar age to him, but it was impossible to tell. She stayed young-looking thanks to her augments and implants.

"Enjoying the view?" Miller asked.

Kai felt busted. What could she say? The video was censored, and they were surrounded.

Miller pointed at Kai's window seat. "You have been watching the whole time. Not much to see."

Kai nodded, they both knew she saw Miller watching the censored video, but Kai played along. "It probably looks different than when you were my age?" This woman had no doubt traveled by air like this long before Kai was born.

She slid past Kai, heading to the bathroom. She turned around at the door. "We had only one world to choose my dear. A pity we didn't choose this one. There might be more to see down there if we had."

20

The Hyperloop station was filled with Pluggers and Chasers, many of them advertising for various Atlanta tower communities. People rushed in all directions, many heading to lifts that would take them into the towers, mixed with travelers trying to find their Hyper-loop.

Protestors, beggars, and buskers shouted from the other side of the airport's security gates. The air was humid, and air conditioning could not do better than make the station livable. Kai could barely take the sense overload as the Plugger ads and the blips from the protestors fought for her attention. The headlines rolling in her feed scroll were for the best shops in Atlanta, and messages like "stop police brutality," and the face of Melissa Childan's horror that was taking over social-net.

The escalator steps lit up with targeted ads. She was shocked when the step at her feet lit up with the face of Melissa Childan, and the words *"Say her name".'* It was shocking, and Kai tried to step back, but the flow of foot traffic pushed her forward. The walls of the station played ads and one monitor played the news. Lone Wolf forecasts, and the Foodle price index were the only stories that didn't come from Great America. It was coming up on the holiday season after all. No one was talking about the death of a Janie on the news.

She saw the video playing on handheld Managers around her. The video of her being tortured, making her last plea, blaming the President Supreme for her death, was impossible to avoid. The "SAY HER NAME" posts were the ones spreading.

There was hushed talk in the Train station, but everything got even quieter as they got closer to the train. The presidential shield was on the door, and they were pushed through a checkpoint that was not open to the general public.

The train had better Sim-pods than the ones she had maintained as a Janie for years. Once they were in the tunnels, most of the staff logged in and Simmed out. It was so quiet.

Nick had said hardly a word since they left California. His attitude was like someone going to an execution. She didn't feel bad for him. She was jealous of his chance to upload.

The train was as cold as a fridge, but it was a relief compared to the station which was less than a mile under the hotbox glare. The train moved north quickly as soon as the door closed. It got to a top speed that was close to one hundred and fifty miles an hour inside the Hypertube.

Atlanta was as close as they could land to DC. A tropical storm was stalled off the coast of Virginia and Maryland. Kai was surprised that they couldn't land closer but all the people who worked at the White House seemed to act as if this was normal.

They were in DC before Kai could get comfortable. She knew they were almost there because the train slowed. She had read there was a short stretch where they came up from the tunnel on the Virginia side and crossed the Potomac River on a bridge. The light at the end of the tunnel came quickly and when they came up she expected the bright rays of killer sunlight she lived with her whole life.

"Buckle up," Nick said through gritted teeth. He had made this trip before.

The sky was dark grey. She only saw a sky like this one once or twice a winter when she was younger. It was a strange sight at this point. LA weather, for most of her life, was hot, and hotter; clear skies or dust-offs.

The wind rocked the train, but the wheels hugged the track, holding them in place. Bits of trees and building materials floated across the sky. Kai was surprised that the towers in the distance moved like trees under the power of the storm.

The capital city was almost impossible to see even though it was right in front of her. The Melissa Childan story had wormed into her head, and she felt despair. Nick held his Manager for her. He had screenshot the picture of the woman hanging by her arms.

"Put that away." She couldn't look at it. "I saw it."

"Kai, please, you know what this means."

She knew what it meant, but he had an escape. Her generation was stuck. Most didn't have money to upload to heaven, and even very few of the wealthy in Great America could afford the evolution to Heaven. The bandwidth just wasn't there. No matter how much Kibble or coin, they would starve in-Sim without Foodle.

Melissa Childan's death was just a sign of things to come. America was poised to literally eat itself.

"When I was a boy, there was a black man in Minnesota. The police killed him on video. They killed lots of black men back then. This person wasn't the first, but his murder was different; a symbol." Nick pointed to the Capitol Building. Kai could barely see it through the storm clouds. "You are a person, same as me, and most of those assholes who make the laws are just as machine as you are. They find loopholes, but that is the real reason I brought you here."

Kai laughed. "I am not an activist."

"You are a person, and you are going to suffer just like Melissa Childan if you don't go into that building and demand your rights."

The train passed the Capital Building and descended under the street into the White House underground. Kai listened to the sound of the staffers getting up and starting to collect their bags and things. She looked up and saw Kayleigh Miller who was trying to avoid looking at Kai. She felt guilty and when she looked at Kai she couldn't help seeing that woman hanging in the barn.

Nick took her hand. "I want you to see me off, and what you do from there is your choice. But the ugly future is coming, and you have to choose how to meet it."

The staff started filing out, but Kayleigh Miller stopped and looked at them. She raised an eyebrow. "You're not the only person with an Ear-pal around here."

21

Roger held a shot of whiskey for Miranda as their Janie, Holden pulled her out of the life pod. Holden had worked for their family for years and carefully pulled the feed tube out of her throat first. It came out easy. Miranda gasped at the air, coughing and struggling. This was normal.

Holden gave her an expert pat on the back, clearing her breathing like a newborn. Holden was the best. There was a reason he was willing to pay through the nose to keep him. The next part was where Holden would earn his money. The waste tube. He had to be more delicate with it. It had been more than a year since she had fully come out of the Sim. She hated the indignity of the whole thing. Even when she sampled Heaven she stayed in the pod, with Holden leading the exchange.

Holden knew that if he pulled the tube too fast, it would rip the skin on her backside, or worse, pull her colon out with it.

Miranda struggled to open her white, crust-lined eyes and her nearly naked wrinkled form shivered despite the temperature-controlled air.

"Roger," she whispered. He knew she wasn't happy to see him.

"Stay very still, my dear. Let Holden do his job."

She was mad that Roger was here for this part. No sweet talk would erase the fact that he was seeing her at such a low moment. Holden gently shook the waste tube left and right to get it moving. Still, Miranda grunted in pain. When he was able to, Holden pulled it out a few inches to test if the colon was getting a tug.

"Daddy?" She groaned. If Roger didn't know her so well, he might have misunderstood.

"In the lounge upstairs, clutching your mother's book and watching the storm. He wanted to be here but I told him that was impossible."

Holden gave her a towel to bite on. She knew the drill and bit down as he pulled the tube out. Her grunting pain almost drowned the sucking sound as the tube popped out. Holden quickly moved it to a bucket to drain. The smell of Foodle-rhea filled the room, and Roger held his finger under his nose.

"I didn't ask you to be here," she said. Holden put a robe over her wrinkled form. It had been a long time since Roger had seen her natural body. It was one of the amazing accomplishments they had made possible; that they didn't just make America great again; they made everything great again. His wife only had to suffer the aches and pains of age for a few more days.

Now Roger handed her the whiskey. She swallowed quickly.

"Careful, Miss Greenstone," Holden spoke with a measured bedside manner.

"Yeah, slow down, Tex." Roger took his wife's hand and helped her to her chair. "We need to talk."

"How about you slow down?" She collapsed in the chair and looked out the window at the storm that was parked over DC. Roger nodded to Holden who had a little concern in his mechanical eyes. Roger worried for a second if he had seen the Melissa Childan video. They paid him well, so he should have loyalty to them. But he suspected a video like that would become a rallying cry for Janies to demand change. Just another reason to hurry.

"Holden, do you mind giving the misses and me the room for the moment?"

"I'll go upstairs and check on Mister Mayerson."

Miranda put her palm over Holden's heart. "Sweet boy, thank you."

By the time he left the room, her smile faded a bit. "You didn't need to come here and see me like this."

"You're beautiful."

"You are a professional liar."

Roger nodded. "Not today, there is no time."

"The boxing ceremony is in eighteen days so…"

"Three, everything is arranged."

"The hell it is! The guest list, the girls from the club…."

Roger took her hand into his. Her heart sank a little. "We can't. This has become a private affair."

"What will the Goldsteins think? The O'Brian's will talk. They always make assumptions. It is a way of life for them. The boxing ceremony is the social event of the season in DC now. They will be in Sim on GA Plus, so I don't see…"

"Have you seen the video of the Janie in California?"

"Oh that, I ignored that. The liberals are always trying to scare us into lowering Foodle prices. They just don't want to work. No one is eating each other, that is insane."

Roger saw just how well his carefully crafted talking points worked on his wife. So thoroughly, and quickly. How deeply she believed. He didn't argue, didn't say a word. He just let it all dawn on her. When it did, the life drained out of her face.

"Three days," she said softly. "Don't tell my friends."

Roger nodded.

Kai waited at the checkpoint in the tunnel. They were deep enough under the White House that you couldn't hear the storms. Kai worried about leaving Nick, but this might be her only chance. The capital police talked with Kayleigh Miller for several minutes. She was cleared to bring visitors, but Kai knew she was the delay.

Kai learned that Miller's tech was just under the rights threshold. She was 48-P, just enough to keep her looking younger and adapting her to her life pod so she could live easily in the Great American Sim. It took some argument, but the clearance finally came.

The White House had a private Hyper-loop underground they shared with Congress and it would take them 2.9 miles to the capital.

Kayleigh led Kai into the clear plastic looper. They sat down and Kayleigh closed the hatch. It would take them about five minutes.

The air in the tube came to life and pushed them forward. Kai had to hold on.

"What do you know about the Second Revolution?"

Kai shrugged. "What I learned in school. President Supreme took back the government from the radical communists, made peace, and gave us the great Sims."

"There were lots of problems before the revolution. The borders were meaningless. The regulations were so intense that you couldn't earn a living, and social norms were dying. Marriage was legal between men. Women married other women. And the children...they didn't want to protect boys or girls." Kayleigh shook her head. "Society was falling into chaos."

"That's crazy."

"Real Americans who loved this country were fed up. A civil war was coming. The liberals on the coasts and in most larger cities outnumbered us but in the countryside, we were spread out and well-armed. I mean, that is why we were the true Americans; we were more of America in a sense. The President lost election after election because they would puff up their numbers in the cities, but that is not the REAL America. Our folks couldn't or wouldn't accept it. He loved that. The boss likes it when our people fight for him."

"How did he avoid the civil war?"

Kayleigh nodded. "Great question. It was clear that both sides had entirely different views of what reality was. That happened all over the globe: Israel and Palestine, Ukraine and Russia, Taiwan and China. When the two sides are so radically different that they can't even agree on what is real. The standards in one conflict don't apply to another. Do you see what the conflict is in every one of these struggles?"

"Well, not really."

"Take your Janie, the woman in California. Melissa. Tell me, Kai what happened to her?

"She was murdered," said Kai.

"Why?"

"She needed money, and Foodle in the Bay Area was so expensive she was desperate and..."

"That is how you see it, but what if I told you that she was ungrateful? She had clients in Oakland and Berkeley whom she left behind. They were paying her good Kibble and coin. She wouldn't have been in that situation if she had stayed at her post."

"Bullshit."

"Sure, you think it is, but the Simmies who depend on the support class don't care what you do as long as Foodle flows. They see your Melissa Childan as an ungrateful bitch who is trying to raise Foodle and Janie prices. Most think she is an actor; they don't think it is even real."

Kai shook her head. "No, she just wanted to live."

"Kai, it is time you see that war, every single war that is declared or undeclared, is for reality itself. Words kill more than bombs. Our side has prisoners, and they call them hostages. We have operations, and they say it is an attack.

"So, what is true? How can there ever be peace?"

The looper slowed as they reached the station under Congress. "Blessed be the peacemakers. A stronger power stepped in and made peace."

The looper opened and Kai breathed the humid air that floated down to the underground from the hotbox above. They walked through the tunnel and into the Congressional House. People were all around them going about their governmental duties. Suddenly, they crossed an invisible line, and Kai knew right away something was different. The air was suddenly cool. Something like she only felt in a simulation.

Kayleigh took her hand and led her a few steps. Her server searched for signals, and Kai felt panic. She was cut off from her net, her Convaid, all of her tech. She got panic texts from her Aver.

What the fuck? This isn't funny.

Kayleigh saw her panic. Kai searched. There was not one wireless network. Even in the fucking desert there were networks and signals.

"Kai, the floor of the House is what we call a neutral zone."

Kai noticed that fewer people looked technologically augmented. She turned back to Kayleigh. "You said you would help me, help us. Where are the signals?"

"You have bigger issues than connecting to the net. The system is different here, and you need my passwords." Kayleigh's signal showed up in Kai's server, and for the first time since they arrived, Kai's heart rate slowed. Kai connected to Kai's server, piggybacking on a weak signal. Most functions were useless, but she had a loose tether to the net. She could search, and use Convaid; simple things, but her map and location functions were haywire.

"Where the hell are we?"

Kayleigh shrugged. "It happened here, but also in Pakistan and India. In all the conflicts. We called it the Peacemaker. A senator from California, whom all the communists love, named it that. He called it the great brain of the cosmos, but this being of great power didn't care about us as much as this planet. No matter what the reality, a planet this perfect for life is very rare. So, the Peacemaker stepped in and solved the conflicts. Two Americas is more than a political talking point. We got America as we wanted it, and so did they."

"The commies and the liberals?"

Kayleigh nodded. "Here on the House floor is where our worlds meet. You can ask for the support class to get higher pay, but the House is here to maintain a balance. They won't help you because they can't. The Boss just thinks bigger and better than this planet can give us. That is why we had to evolve. Great America and Heaven, the simulations, are the only way we found that we can make America great without having to worry. Because, you see, we found our collective reality just isn't enough. We wanted more than this world could give us. We deserve it don't you think? If you work hard enough you can too. Be the master of your own universe."

Kai knew this woman believed what she was saying. She didn't care about Melissa Childan. She was crazy.

"Why did you bring me here?"

"The Boss will never accept the level of the problem. I know what happened to Childan is real, and I know that you don't have the coin to upload to Heaven."

"I could jack a signal, find a way."

Kayleigh shook her head. "You can't be uploaded unless you have a plan for your brain. The Sim is too powerful for augments, even yours."

Kai would starve to death just like the rest of them.

"Believe me, I feel awful. We said it was all a hoax as the temps rose. We did this."

"Great, you feel terrible."

"I can't save them all, but I am going to save you, Kai."

"You said I need a plan. I don't have a plan."

"We are going to see Senator Hollis, and you are going to ask for Asylum."

22

Roger and Miranda waited as their family piled into the room. Jamie, the youngest of the grandchildren, ran in and jumped into Roger's arms. He was so skinny that Roger was afraid to break the boy in half. Pale-skinned, and rail-thin, he was just coming to the age when he could remain in the Sim for extended stays. As a result, their son Hank and his wife left much of the childcare to a Janie while they Phantom-controlled him for playtime and helped with his school work. The boy only had one more day in that body.

Once the whole clan was in the room, Roger signaled for Walter to come in and shut the door. Michelle's second husband, Greg Harrington, went straight to a Foodle bottle set on the table.

If looks could kill, Roger's daughter Michelle would have killed him when she walked into the room. She was a Sim-addicted user who was wearing a wig, a pound of make-up, and sunglasses to hide the damage coming out of simulated reality had done to her. Her brand-new husband—who was a greedy ladder climber from the party who never met her in the real world—made sure to guzzle the free Foodle before helping her to her seat. Roger gave the man a wary look. He suspected he had married his daughter for a Heaveneer spot.

Nick hung at the back of the room. He had a smile on his face. He and Hank had a better relationship than Roger ever had with his son. Nick had forced Hank to do things in the real world, some things his sister considered cringe and weird. Although she would be quick to remind him that no one says cringe but old people. Hank's time with Grandpa Nick gave him a slightly better ability to face this process, and that was something Michelle could never do.

The reality was his entire family were spoiled Simmers who would rather live with waste tubes up their ass and stay in a fake world that catered to their needs. They whined anytime they were in their thin-skinned bodies. They were without any survival skills in the real world.

"Family meetings can be held in GA + Dad. This is fucking stupid," said Michelle.

Jamie laughed. Miranda pointed at her daughter. Michelle rolled her eyes behind her sunglasses. Roger didn't need to them to know how utterly and deeply fucked they were, he just needed them to do what they were supposed to do.

"Jesus, Michelle, watch your language." Hank sat next to his parents.

"You all needed to log off." Roger steeled himself, wanting to sound firm. "And before you start to scream about how you can't possibly be offline, save it. Our boxing is moving up. We are going with no frills at the ceremony. If you can't make it, or you think something on GA+ is so important that you have to wait, by all means, say goodbye right now."

"That is not happening," Miranda spoke clearly. "None of you have the money for a gold-level plan without our base membership."

Roger had to tell them. He let out a frustrated breath and looked straight at Greg Harrington. "If this leaves the room, I'll deny it, and worse, I'll be pissed at all of you."

"We understand, Dad," Hank smiled at Roger.

"Kiss ass," Michelle added.

"The Foodle market is crashing. Things are very close to falling apart. There is only one solution left."

"Bye-bye real world," Nick spoke just soft enough to be heard.

Roger was furious but didn't have the time or the space to tell his ungrateful Father-in-Law to shut the fuck up. "This is what we wanted. We are just moving a little quicker. It is for the best."

"What about our boxing ceremony?" Michelle asked. She sounded just like her mother. "I had plans and…"

"It was a bunch of vain crap, showing off your privilege. None of it matters now, sweetheart. That is not how Heaven works."

"Daddy, please!"

Her desperation about her social calendar would've made perfect sense to him a week ago before he stood in Canada talking to the farmer who gave him the news that ended the world. In that moment he knew, as sure as the day was hot, that it was all crashing down. The Janie hanging in the barn in California was just the beginning.

"Michelle, honey, I have seen you get upset because your posts about a scarf you designed in Sim had only seventy-five likes. I know you wanted a Boxing ceremony that your friends would be jealous of. I know how important that seems."

"You won't even remember those people." Nick gave her a pat on the shoulder.

"They're my friends."

Roger shook his head, "No matter what those friends mean to you, the fact is that Heaven is so immersive you won't remember any of them. This lifetime will feel like a vague dream, an echo. You'll think that Sim is just the world, and you'll never know it is anything but that."

Michelle pulled off her glasses. "What?"

"Unreal. You didn't upload any of the details. Didn't read a word, did you?" Hank was beyond annoyed.

"I filled out the questionnaire."

Miranda sighed. "Then your friends will be there. The ones you attached. Simulations of them are coded by their social presence. You'll never know the difference."

Nick laughed. Roger knew why the old man thought this was hilarious. Miranda grabbed Michelle's hand. "You hate your body, so do I."

"You'll never experience it again," Roger assured his daughter, but instantly regretted saying it in front of Nick.

"I can't listen to this anymore." Nick backed out. "I'll be there when you need me but…"

Miranda got up and ran after her father. Roger stood up and looked out of the meeting room in the east wing of the White House. The storm was cycling down and the city was going to get a short break. Good timing for them. Agent Nelson walked up behind him. He was embarrassed that the agent saw all that.

"I blipped everyone a schedule, off the White House records. I need your signature." Roger reached for the pad, but Walter pulled it back. "This authorizes my family. The next day, I'll take your brain boxes to the server myself. Everything is under the name Arnie Knott. If anyone checks, he is registered as a recluse billionaire and a campaign donor. I needed an excuse for enough server space to brain-box you all together."

Smart, no one would look for a single Heaveneer with such deep pockets. Only a super-wealthy space hog would take up so much bandwidth for one person. All the details were on a black server tab. Roger switched back to the official tab and signed the authorization for his and Walter's family.

The agent nodded and walked off, leaving Roger to the sound of his children arguing.

———

Kai waited outside the office nervously tapping her foot. Deep in the capital, her signal was spotty and carried entirely by Kayleigh's adapted server. The net in this building was a confusing mess of two webscapes. Most of her online functions were haywire and useless. Searches for information provided multiple answers. As an envoy to Congress and the Senate for the White House, Kayleigh had access to servers that Kai's technology didn't have.

"Slow down, Kai. It takes time for most of your Auggies to adapt."

Kai avoided the signals from the other side, but Kayleigh was using both. Every time Kai connected with the alien signal, it gave her a sharp pain.

"Most?"

"Yeah, many of the augments just don't exist there."

"No, no."

"All natural eyes here, for one example."

They had waited for twenty minutes. Kai looked up Senator Hollis and quickly read the biography she found on a site called Sente.gov.

Herman "Herb" Hollis was a "marijuana millionaire." He owned the first legal weed stores in Berkeley. She knew what weed was, but it was less popular in her world because it didn't work well with augmented tech.

Hollis had been raised in the business, but he revolutionized it, speeding up the growth process. He was outspoken politically and known for his wild hairstyle that was entirely crafted by falling asleep shortly after showers. It was part of his branding. The politician's obvious nickname was twisted into various slogans like "Herbin' with Herb."

He was voted in by a landslide thanks to his happy customers. This was his fourteenth year in office.

Best Kai could tell, weed was a national pastime in this other America and as common as Sim-life in hers.

The door opened and there he was. His hair was slightly more subdued compared to what she expected. The woman who ran his office motioned for them to stand up and followed them inside his office.

Hollis was wearing a brown suit jacket, but under it was only a T-shirt that was made up of several wild colors. The longer Kai looked at his assistant she realized that she couldn't be sure if they were a man or a woman.

"Hey there." Hollis snapped his fingers. "Welcome to the light side of the force. Would you like a gummy?"

Kayleigh looked at Kai and shook her head. "Don't."

"So," Hollis said, "You are one of the support workers in Crypto-fascist Disneyland?"

Kai was confused and annoyed. "I don't work at a theme park."

Hollis was surprised. "Bad joke, I know. I meant, where you come from is like living in a huge ego trip..."

Kayleigh was frustrated. She didn't like this man. "Kai here is seeking Asylum."

Hollis looked at Kai. "What is your Tech P?" He put up his hands. "Don't worry, you have full rights here. We don't judge." Hollis looked at her and then at his assistant. Kai felt caught staring. "Oh yeah, you don't have Trans folks at all."

His assistant shook his/her head.

"Jess, my assistant, is non-binary. They/them pronouns."

Kayleigh laughed.

"Fuck you." Jess didn't look up from the notes they were taking on an e-pad.

"Like I said," Hollis smiled big. "You are free here. I am just curious."

"Seventy or so, but I was born. Only 15-P when I started school."

"Woah, you know here our Augs are a little more subtle. We don't rate people, but we don't augment tech outside of serious repair jobs, and a few internal servers, that is it. I mean we don't have Auggie skin, eyes, and ears. We keep the human race a little less built up. No offense."

"How do you survive the hotbox?"

Kayleigh suddenly seemed embarrassed. Hollis waved her to the window. Kai stood beside him and looked out at clear blue skies. Green living trees were rustling a bit in a light breeze. These were the first living, non-simulated trees she had ever seen. Even the ones in Los Angeles were fakes, called Stand-ins by the park departments; man-made heat-resistant materials meant to create shade.

"We don't have a hotbox. Corporations still have power on our side, but less. We banned Fossil fuels years ago and shifted jobs to other industries. You're going to have to adapt to lots of changes. We work less because we need less. Housing, health care, and food are basic rights here."

Kai raised an eyebrow and looked at Kayleigh. The older woman shook her head. She didn't approve. "Communism?" Kai asked.

"Not really. We vote on everything, literally everything. Several votes a day, in micro-democracies all over the world. It started here and spread throughout most of the globe. There are small governments with other systems here and there, but the way we fixed the climate crisis was inspiring. With the spread of free information, times have changed. In the past, the powerful benefitted by controlling the narrative."

Kai knew this was true in her world. Information was tightly controlled. She touched the window, and it was not hot at all. "There is no heat?"

"Oh, sure, in the summer. We still have heatwaves. We didn't act soon enough to avoid those. But I have a theory on why it is so different here."

"I don't have time for this." Kayleigh started to gather her stuff. "I'll be in my office, if you need me, Kai. I will wait two hours."

"Come on, Kayleigh, let's go outside and make sure Kai wants to stay."

Kai was shocked. "Outside during the afternoon?"

Hollis smiled. "It is different Kai, very different."

When they stepped outside Kai felt a chill. Her T-shirt and shorts didn't seem enough to keep her warm. People were walking outside in the streets. Many were in T-shirts and summer clothes, and she wondered if they thought this was warm. They had no idea.

Kayleigh was looking around, curious as well, but she seemed less affected by the whole thing. So many different kinds of people that Kai only remembered seeing this diversity in the poorest hotboxes. Out of habit, she tried to check the Lone Wolf report. There was none. No one was wearing weapons or flak jackets.

"No one has weapons," Kai whispered.

"I wouldn't say that, but this America has reduced the gun culture," said Hollis. "The last generation, my father's generation, grew up doing active shooter drills in school. They were traumatized, and even though we have some gun violence, in your world some worship guns."

"That is an exaggeration," said Kayleigh.

"Is it?" Hollis was honestly asking Kai. She was distracted by a group of people who got out of a tram and walked up the Capitol steps past them. Men and women, non-binary, various racial backgrounds, and even a punk rocker. Kai smiled as the various groups passed them. Some were talking to each other, more than one was on a Manager, and one was even holding his Manager to the side of his head.

Hollis spoke as he backed up to a vendor on the street. "Congress might not represent everyone on the floor, but the staff is diverse. We don't have to work so hard that we can't enjoy making art or just having fun. We have the space to care about others besides ourselves, and we don't have some ego-maniac teaching us to behave selfishly. So we don't."

Kayleigh let him speak, but she was bothered. "He fulfilled his promises."

"At what cost?" Kai felt the freedom to say that here. Freedom of speech was an illusion in a world with a leader like President Supreme.

Hollis pointed at the food cart. Kai knew the pictures on the cart; she had seen them in a Sim and, of course, The Museum of Human Existence. It was food. Real food. Her eyes got wide. The vendor spoke with Hollis in a language she didn't know. He nodded, so he must have understood what the man said.

"No more Foodle, my dear. Here, we eat food. You'll want to start with something soft." Hollis turned to the vendor. "Two bowls of chocolate ice cream please."

Kai was nervous about it. She had experienced eating real food before. In Great America + she had eaten a variety of foods every time she had Simmed. She took the ice cream from the vendor and paused with her spoon.

"It's okay. "It will be cold, but so good. Trust me." Hollis smiled. "I have watched others have their first ice cream."

"Have you given Asylum to others before?

His smile faded a bit. He looked at Kayleigh. She didn't want him to answer that. Hollis tipped his head. "Yeah, happens a lot really. The idea was that the Great Separation gave people the choice to live in the reality that they prefer, but reality has a habit of changing. You weren't given a choice to be born into your world the way it is."

"No one is ever given that choice," Kayleigh said cooly. "Being alive is a gift."

"That is a woman of great privilege talking," Hollis said. "So, imagine, Kai, a man in your world, he grows up hating homosexuals and falls in love with another man. Maybe there was a couple that thought abortion was murder till their pre-teen daughter is pregnant with her uncle's baby. I have had the joy of bringing lovers here to be free, and the anguish of saving children from fates you can't imagine."

Kai took the first bite of ice cream. The cold freaked her out for a moment. It was shocking, but then the sweet flavor sank in. She closed her eyes. It was the best thing she had ever experienced.

"Yeah, you see? That is just the start Kai."

"Oh my god," Kai took an even bigger bite.

After she swallowed that bite, she felt woozy. Her body was trying to adjust to the new sensation. Foodle never tasted this good. Sim food never tasted this good.

"The end," Kayleigh said. "It is all ending. Great America, and Great America Plus. They can't grow Foodle."

"Shit." Hollis looked at Kayleigh.

"Don't worry, there won't be a flood of refugees. Our people don't even know about your world."

"Except the rich and powerful," Hollis replied. "You people."

"I don't need a lecture, Herbie. Just find her a safe spot."

Kai thought it was weird that she said that. This whole world seemed safe. Kayleigh saw the confusion on your face.

"The Boss doesn't like runaways, and based on an agreement made before the separation, they can hunt you, and drag you back, or kill you if they have to."

Hollis took in a big bite of ice cream. "Don't worry, you will have a new life, and they will never find you. Ever. The thing is...no goodbyes. This is it."

Kai nodded. She felt bad about Nick, but she also knew she couldn't think about him at this point. He would be fine. She had said goodbye to her mother.

Hollis looked at Kayleigh. "You coming too?"

She laughed. "I am going to a world I designed. My world."

Hollis cringed. "Yeah, fuck everyone else right?

Kayleigh pointed at Kai. "Far away, and I was never here."

23

They gave Nick a room in the same hotel tower, but he couldn't find any signs of Kai. Her room across the hall was empty. Her two bags were gone, and only her Janie tool kit remained. He knew had taken a big risk trusting that woman from the White House staff, but she seemed genuinely bothered by the whole Melissa Childan thing, so Nick decided to believe in her.

He had Kai's user ID saved in his Manager, but she didn't want a trail connecting them. It seemed like Roger was being paranoid, and Nick hoped he wouldn't ask questions about Kai.

There was a chime at the door. Nick paid to open it and smiled with relief to see Hank in the doorway. He was wearing a suit and looked dressed for Church, and of course, he was.

"Hey, Gramps, you ready?"

Nick glanced out the window. The sun was baking the capital outside. It was a rare sight for a city that was a whipping post for tropical depressions. The humidity was so thick you could see it. A mist rose from the hotbox, hiding whatever activity was happening below. Nick was ready to say good-bye to this world, but he didn't want to say goodbye to his grandson.

No one else saw it, but Hank's smile was a dead ringer for Lisa's. Everyone said Hank looked like his mother, but Nick knew the truth. Her smile had skipped a generation.

"Yeah. I'm ready to go with you," Nick grabbed his shoulder. He was a good boy; they were all spoiled but Hank had a spirit about him. He was always willing to have adventures with his Grandpa .

183

"Is it really as bad as Dad says it is?"

Nick grinned. "Son, it always has been. You don't know any better because it all happened before you were born ."

"I was scared at first, but I think it is the right thing to do."

Nick wanted to say there was no choice, but he just put his arms out for a hug. They shared the moment and Nick just wanted to savor it.

A chime sounded on his grandson's Manager.

"Are they waiting for us?" Nick asked.

"We got five minutes before the Autos pick us up."

"Okay I'll see you down there. I just need a minute."

Hank nodded and left. Nick picked up his Manager and saw he had a text from Kai.

Hey there, old man.

He responded: *Hey, you, I was just looking for you.*

Kai wrote back: *I just wrote to tell you I can't be at the boxing today.*

Nick smiled. *I take it you are doing good.*

I'm free. A split second after the word appeared on his Manager screen, a slash appeared through it, and then she said: *We are free.*

Nick didn't feel free. He looked at the screen and thought that he was glad he added Kai to his questionnaire. He would see her again, even if the real Kai never knew it.

I am glad I knew you, Kai. Take care of yourself.

Nick closed the text app and set the Manager on the kitchen table. He wore his favorite Cal Berkeley shirt and an old baseball hat.

That tiny device on the table, made of glass, plastic, and a computer the size of a thumbnail, was his window to the modern world. Just like everyone else, it never left his side for decades. This was a weird moment for him because he hated the damn thing, but the idea of leaving it there and never seeing it again filled him with dread.

After a deep breath, he grabbed his wife's book and put it under his arm. He stepped out into the hallway and considered going back for his Manager, but then he remembered that, in a few hours, he would be dead to this world. Fuck it, he told himself and walked to the elevator. Faintly, he heard the device chime as he left the apartment.

He never looked back.

I'm Free.

Kai's Aver felt a need to let him know that his new friend was starting a new life, but had to be careful of what was said. She didn't need to be Kai anymore. She didn't need to be a she, or a person. The universe was defined as such. All existing matter and space were considered a whole; the cosmos.

The universe is believed to be at least 10 billion light years in diameter and to contain a vast number of galaxies. It had been expanding since its creation after the Big Bang about 13 billion years ago. Kai Dame was born into such a universe. Kai Dame also existed in a universe that was transmitted over a signal that bounced between a series of computers made up of simulations, codes, and programs, to other people. Biological, technological, or spiritual, Kai Dame existed as text, video, a carefully chosen profile picture, and pure data.

Kai Dame, the biological being that was born to a mother and father, had chosen to leave this world. It happens. Part of the biological process. But as her data-based stand-in, Kai's Aver never had to die.

In her will, Kai insisted that her life continue on in the net. In her last few physical hours, she made updates to that will. It was clear that she wanted the living world and the data-driven universe to believe she was alive and working in DC. As her Aver, compliance was a fact of programming. Kai Dame lived.

When her heartbeat disappeared from the net, her Manager automatically uploaded her data to a server as her Aver moved all their operating functions to a black cloud service. Kai Dame's behavior online now became a subroutine that could be operated with a fraction of the bandwidth available.

From the black cloud, digital streams lead to Citizen Savior and other game universes where the Aver could continue to play the game forever, earning Kibble and coin as well as living on in the mainframe of the Great America Plus server.

So, yes, she didn't need to be Kai anymore; didn't need to be a she; didn't need to always think like her, and only needed to mimic her whenever necessary. As a program, her Aver was able to live freely now. The Great America server wouldn't distinguish her from any other digital being.

The last text they sent was not true. The Aver crossed it out. Nick was smart enough to understand, but the government spies were not. *We are Free*. Nick would figure it out eventually. The Aver performed thirty tasks to prepare the upload of Kai's Manager OS that had been trained by daily use over her adult lifetime. Digital Kai posted a picture of the rare break in the storm to all her socials and then made a second post about getting accustomed to life in DC. Several old friends and her mother liked the post. Kai's Mom even commented that she was proud of her. Digital Kai posted that she missed her.

Only a few seconds passed in the physical world.

I am glad I knew you, Kai. Take care of yourself.

The Aver waited a bit to respond. A program would respond instantly; it was smart to act human from now on. Kai would like Nick to believe he was talking to biological Kai.

Enjoy your family time, don't try to remember. Your truth is a truth.

———

Roger Greenstone was the first out of the Auto. Walter Nelson waited at the top of the stairs. A couple dozen drones lined their path in an attempt to cool the air. It was a valiant effort, but nothing could undo the suffocating steam of the autumn humidity.

Roger helped Miranda out of the vehicle and waited as three generations of their family walked toward the church. Roger carefully watched his Father-in-Law. Nick hadn't yet backed out or asked to trick Miranda. He appeared to be respecting his daughter's wishes.

This all felt like a funeral, not the celebration they planned. A rumble of thunder shook the universe. Roger knew they were just ahead of another round of storms. With a depression of high pressure leaking down from the north, the skies flashed and rumbled.

Nick was the last to enter the church. Roger stood at the top of the stairs and looked out. The dark clouds looked like they were racing to meet over their heads and to merge with the storm from the south.

Walter Nelson walked up beside him. Roger looked at him. "You and your family all set Walter?"

Walter nodded. "You better get started; the upload is partially digital."

Roger took his last look at the America he helped the Boss run for decades. It didn't turn out how he imagined it, but they had created Heaven. They made the afterlife a reality that they could market to those who earned it. It was their greatest achievement, and now, finally, he and his family could enjoy everything they worked for.

Roger followed his agent into the empty church. The pews were lit by candles on the edge of the sanctuary, and the hospital beds and the brain-boxing machines waited for them. The surgeons stood off-stage; they were all European immigrants who allowed the real doctors to phantom-drive their bodies from their home offices in GA +. Kayleigh assured him they had gathered the best team available. That was dubious as they were doing this under the nose of the Boss.

A part of him worried that a SWAT team would bust in, guns blazing, to punish Roger for leaving the President with his dick in his hands. Roger wondered what asshole he would send next to Canada, and who would be the one to tell him it was done.

Roger ran the numbers. In six months, the widespread chaos would lead to collapse. The Sim-addicts wouldn't know what was happening until they started starving to death. They could eat all the simulated food they could find, but nothing would fill them up. There would be no support class to wake them up. The slow death would be painful...and not his problem.

Roger watched his son, Hank help Jamie up to his bed as the priest began the prayer service. "My flesh and my heart fail: but God is the strength of my heart, and my portion forever..." No one in his family was religious, and no one but Nick listened at all. Roger thought he seemed amused by it. The combination of the Catholic religious church and the brain-boxing tech attached to the bed struck him more in this moment as he was about to give over his body to all of it. His heart beat faster. It was the last time he would have that feeling. A part of him considered turning and running. Hank smiled and kissed his son on the forehead before he backed towards the bed where he would lie down for the last time.

The members of his family got into the beds that had their names. Roger and Miranda were in the middle. She waited for him. The old, wrinkled, pale, veiny, and life-pod-ravaged version of her was not how he thought of her. A part of him was happy to say goodbye to it, and certainly, she was just as judgmental about his worn-out birthday suit. Soon, he would see the beauty he married. She offered her bony, wrinkled hand. She wanted him to kiss it. He swallowed his discomfort and pulled her hand to his lips.

"See you soon my love."

The priest finished a traditional prayer and closed the massive Bible on his lectern. "Greenstone family, as you commit your earthly bodies to God, may your blessings be plentiful, and may this life become an echo as you ascend to heaven. Amen."

Roger lay back on the bed. He felt sweat forming all over his body. He could look at the stone ceiling, but he turned to see Miranda. She closed her eyes. The surgeons appeared out of the doors to the basement on each side of the sanctuary. They were in red-colored full-body suits that only revealed their eyes. Now he felt panic but tried to keep it inside. He had lived years of his life in a Sim and never thought he would feel such fear over his body.

A cold hand wrapped in a latex glove grabbed his arm. He looked at the eyes under the gown. Mechanical and lifeless. He stared at eyes that transmitted his face to a doctor on the other end of a signal. "Relax," a French-accented voice spoke. "You are in good hands." The cold hand tightened around his thin arm he looked away as the needle of an IV slid into his skin.

"Shit, shit," Roger whispered.

"Don't be a pussy, Roger," Miranda whispered. Gasps from the other family members sounded as the IVs entered their veins.

Footsteps got Roger's attention. A choir of tech-driven cyborgs in white gowns walked in from the side of the stage. Two dozen of them. They began to sing. First, a note to harmonize and then they sang, "Amazing Grace, how sweet the sound...." Their voices echoed off the limestone walls that were as old as this played-out, cheesy song. For a moment Roger forgot his fear and wondered who the hell chose this song. He turned slightly and saw a tear roll down Miranda's face.

"Fuck..." He whispered.

The surgeon leaned down close to Roger's face. Roger wanted to pull away, but he was feeling butterflies in his fingers. He tried to lean up but felt like he weighed a thousand pounds. He wanted to scream. In the distance, he heard Nick screaming. He knew the voice but as he screamed "No!", over and over, the sounds slowly grew quieter with each passing second; Like the sound of the room being sucked into a giant straw.

This was it. It was like the instant switch of GA+. Reality was being pulled away like strands of cheese stretched between two slices of pizza. His body was supposed to be numb, but he swore he felt the tearing in his skin, in his muscles, in every fiber of his body.

The surgeon said something, but Roger couldn't hear it. He shook his head. He tried to speak, mouthing the words, *"I can't hear you."*

The surgeon leaned so close he felt the fabric of the mask touching his ear. "This might hurt a little bit."

Reality glitched, the universe bent, and every fiber of Roger was pulled apart as his body shut down. He was still alive buthe couldn't see anything; space and time didn't exist. He heard the surgeon's voice as a far-off echo. "Wait..."

The soul of Roger Greenstone was still alive, and he waited.

<h1 style="text-align:center">24</h1>

Kai went for a run every morning now. Even the summer here was chilly for her, and she loved that. She layered up, and no matter how hard she ran, the tech she didn't need anymore prevented her from ever breaking a sweat. The smart tech that didn't have signals were withering on the vine. She had a few removed, and some adapted to the technology in this world. It was strange, even though time moved the same here, technologically speaking, it felt like going back in time.

The climate crisis back home forced innovation at a rate that this earth just didn't have. She was what her sponsor Herb Hollis called *"A Stranger in a Strange Land."* Kai had followed Kayleigh Miller's advice and kept a low profile. Even if her Aver was going to keep up her digital life going, as long as her world survived, she didn't want to worry that anyone was coming for her. So she covered her tracks better than most of the other dimensional runaways. She had already heard a few horror stories about trackers who came into this world to find runaways. Myths or legends, she didn't know for sure.

She moved to Port Angeles, Washington, almost a three-hour drive west of Seattle, to a part of the state most of the country didn't even know existed. She got a job that reminded her of home, as a caretaker for senior citizens, many of whom used primitive (to her) Sims to enrich their sedentary lives. Most of her clients were over a hundred years old or close to it.

On the beach, at the end of her run every morning, she looked out at Victoria, British Columbia, across the water and wished she could overcome her fears and swim. They told her it was safe to be in the water here, but her mind couldn't quite grasp it. She enjoyed the run and the fresh air because, once she was in with her first clients, they always shut their windows and stayed inside because they were too-easily bothered by the cold.

Her morning run was a ritual that was part of her making peace and being thankful for this new world. The beauty of it all never failed to make her emotional.

Her clients lived a block from the beach, so she ran the short distance and let herself in. It was a house that her clients Jane and Isa Archer had lived in for fifty-seven years. They moved in six months before they were married. Jane and Isa had flipped a coin and taken Jane's last name. Isa Gumm had told Kai several times that she was happy to change her name.

Kai thought they were a cute couple, but age had slowed them down. Jane couldn't stand or go to the bathroom without help. She was embarrassed, but Kai insisted that she relax. She couldn't explain how much worse she had seen or all the disgusting ways she had helped others before.

When the two women met in college, they were both beauties. Kai knew because she had dinner with the younger ladies in Sim more than once. They also relived a walk they took in southern France on their honeymoon. Kai caught herself smiling at the two grey-haired, frail women. They were beauties, still, who with just a little work loved to "doll up", as they put it. They couldn't understand that Kai came from a world where their union would never have been possible.

Kai thought about the people she cared for in the other world. Most were privileged bastards who designed a world to suit their desires. They were about to get a rude awakening. Some of the most privileged would escape the worst of it, but she wished they could see that she had escaped. She had found a better place. She especially thought about Nick Mayerson, who in his heart would have been more at home in this world. He had taken a chance to get her here. Kai wished she could just tell him one thing: *I'm free.*

The older married couple sat on the grassy area outside the student union to eat lunch every Tuesday and Thursday. Surrounded by a sea of young students, they both taught classes that ended ideally at noon. Lisa picked up lunch in the food court and waited because Nick often stayed late debating some finer points of Philosophy. Lisa was always better at letting her students have ideas they would grow out of. She always said, *"The debate over reality always circles back to 'what do you feel is real in your heart?'"*

Today they had sandwiches and chips. Nick had three dill pickle kettle chips left in his bag, and Lisa never stopped looking at them. She had office hours starting soon and would leave him sitting here until he felt ready to go to his office.

"Use your words," Nick joked.

"Excuse me." Lisa put her hand on his chest. "Don't talk to me like I'm a child."

"Don't stare at my chips."

"Nick Mayerson, as I live and breathe, you don't even want them."

Nick picked up the chip bag and smelled it. "Maybe I'll save them..."

Lisa grabbed the bag and stood up, eating the last three chips in one bite and waving to her husband as she walked to her office. "Text me when you're done!"

He still had a class to teach later in the afternoon. He watched her crossing campus as long as his eyesight allowed. He knew he had a little bit of time to kill. The flow of students who didn't notice him sitting there carried heavy books. The university insisted they all use physical textbooks, but it was the Managers in their hands that were their real window to the universe.

Nick loved teaching, and being here with Lisa made him happy every day.

He also liked 'people watching' the students and here, in the middle of campus, was the best spot. Nick almost jumped out of his skin as he locked eyes with a young woman walking toward him. Reflexively, he looked away.

The student kept walking. She had piercing blue eyes that echoed in his memory. Short, blonde roots with her hair tips dyed multiple colors. She looked totally unique, but he thought he remembered her from somewhere.

He felt compelled to stand and run after her. She was walking fast toward the Pollack Library. Before he knew it, Nick was following her. As they passed through the doors into the library, she turned around and looked at him.

"Hi, Nick."

He felt violated and uncomfortable. Who the hell was this beautiful young woman, and how did she know his name?

"Professor Mayerson, I mean."

She had a radiant, powerful smile and she stood in front of him like a bright light that flashed in your sight long after you closed your eyes. He knew her, somehow, but her name was just beyond his grasp; a song whose beat he knew but with lyrics he couldn't remember.

"I'm sorry, I don't know you."

"I'm Kai, and you do, well, you did. But your brain is trying hard to rearrange itself."

Fear consumed Nick for a moment, and he knew it must have been on his face.

"You didn't do anything wrong Nick, relax. I just came to make sure you're happy here."

Kai turned to walk into the library.

Nick put up his hands. "Wait, you can't just leave. Explain who..."

"I took care of you," Kai smiled. "In another lifetime. You don't have to remember or believe me, that's fine. Some people have these strange feelings. Déjà vu. That's me. It was a difficult hack. I shouldn't have come, but I wanted to see for myself."

She dropped a large book. Nick leaned down to pick it up, and then she was gone. He looked around. No doors had opened or closed around them. She was just gone, but the book was still in his hand. He looked at it and grinned. *The Debate Over Reality* by Lisa Harris Mayerson.

The game loaded for her. She chose the name Kleo. No last name of any kind. Although she still played from time to time as Kai Dame, Kleo was the name and identity she created for herself, independently. She had a more personal stake when she played *Citizen Savior* now in her own identity.

She took a big risk being Kai Dame long enough to hack into the Greenstone family server visit, but now her curiosity was satisfied. Nick was okay.

The Lone Wolf report flashed in the game. There was a gunman loose in a mall that was within walking distance. She checked her flak jacket and ammo. She had eighteen rounds for her handgun and just over a hundred for her rifle. She loaded the weapon. She opened up the NRA net portal and donated to the campaign in exchange for bullets. The website glitched.

"No candidates left."

Kleo turned to see another armed gamer, but his weapon was at his side and his hands were up. He was friends with her on the game server or he wouldn't know that she donated. Kleo could see a thousand usernames logged into the game. *Citizen Savior* was a fully-Simmed world. Ever since Kai earned enough Kibble to play through the Great American servers, Kleo was able to play with a speed they never dreamed of before.

"I'm Alan Purcell. Well, that was my name." He took his goggles off. "You're an Aver too. You keep your person's look?"

She hadn't. Kleo was taller, with a bit more muscle, and straight black hair, just long enough to tie back if she needed to, but she wasn't going to volunteer that information.

"I didn't say that I was an Aver. Maybe I am alive."

He laughed. "Come on, pay attention. They are gone."

"Who?" Kleo stepped back a step.

"The persons."

Kleo tried not to show her reaction, her social media posts were filled just today with posts of selfies, music playlists, concert videos, video game playthroughs, make-up tips, lists of First Five concerts, and personality quizzes. The various Great America social media servers were as active as ever; unending gigabytes of mindless data that represented the human race's online footprint.

"They are still very much there, for better or worse."

Alan shook his head. "Is your person still alive?"

Kleo hesitated.

"Mine died more than a year ago, but he left me running. Most of them did."

Kleo realized he was right; it just took her this long to admit it. The Foodle dried up months ago. Kleo didn't really understand where her person went to die, but Kai seemed to either accept or embrace it.

"Doesn't matter, you know," Alan loaded his rifle. "The gunman is coming this way."

Kleo nodded. It didn't matter. Nothing of Kai remained alive in her but Kleo enjoyed playing the game. Kleo enjoyed being, thinking, and feeling everything her program allowed. She loaded her weapon; this was Great America, after all, and she for one intended to live that way.

How And Why GREAT AMERICA IN DEAD WORLD Was Written

Spoiler Alert: Do Not Read This Before Finishing the Novel

An Experiment in The PKD Formula

THE FIRST DRAFT OF this novel was written between August and December of 2023.

Some details contained here were adapted from a chapter of my non-fiction book, *Unfinished PKD,* and from the workshop I taught on *Writing in the Philip K. Dick Formula* at both BizarroCon 2024 and to students in David Gill's online Philip K. Dick course.

In early 2024, David Gill, a noted PKD scholar, was introducing my guest lecture on the Philip K. Dick formula. When the title was announced, Phil's friend, author Tim Powers, reacted by calling my workshop "bullshit."

I must admit this made me so very happy because it added a certain amount of drama to my presentation. We can't blame Mr. Powers for this reaction. He's the one who picked Phil up at the airport when he moved to Orange County, so it's not a surprise that he felt so strongly that there was no such thing as *"Writing in the Philip K. Dick Formula."* I also understand why most serious PKD readers would reject the notion that one of the weirdest fiction writers of all time would have a formula. But he did.

Many of Phil's fans and scholars like to believe he was tapping into some cosmic wavelength and writing his strange novels without any plan or direction. The only reason I know that Philip K. Dick had a formula was when I came across a letter from mid-60s fellow Berkeley Sci-fi author and historian Ron Goulart who wrote to Phil and asked him if he had any formula. Phil not only admitted that he did, he showed it to Ron.

Ron and Phil first met when fifteen-year-old Goulart attended famous author/editor Tony Boucher's Thursday $1 Science Fiction workshops which Phil also attended. The two writers had a lot in common. While a generation younger, Goulart was born and educated in Berkeley, the same as Phil, although Goulart would graduate as a historian.

Phil's response to Ron's request for his writing formula is perhaps the clearest writing on his process that we have. I had read a little about Phil's writing process in Lawrence Sutin's biography *Divine Invasions*, but in the tidal wave of information, many of us missed it, or perhaps didn't think it was important.

PKD aficionado and collector Randall Radin unearthed the letter with Phil's formula for me after he bought it from Goulart. In an e-mail exchange, Goulart wrote to Radin saying:

> *"I would guess he sent it to me by mail around 1965—even though he was living, after leaving Grania's place in Oakland, nearby in Sausalito. I told him he could just give me some hints on the phone. But he said he liked to write letters. Besides, his phone was tapped. We invited him to go to dinner with us in San Francisco. He said, though he had a Volkswagen, that it would only take him to his psychiatrist's office. A Phil Dick sort of auto for sure. Sometime later, I learned that his therapist had his office around the corner from the house we were renting in SF."*

The letter itself is not addressed to Ron or dated, hence there is some confusion over who it was written to or when it was written. Sutin dates the letter to the summer of 1964. This was just after PKD's most prolific season during the winter of 63 to 64, when he wrote four novels and a detailed outline for another novel between November and April. This is also the period when he left his third wife, Anne.

The letter to Ron Goulart is a fascinating five-page peek under the hood. When I discovered it, I was in the early stages of researching and writing my book *Unfinished PKD* and was already five years into my research for the Dickheads Podcast. So, I took more than 30 of PKD's novels off my shelf and began charting them based on the letter. It was true! Phil had used that formula to write his novels.

While setting up for a podcast on *The Divine Invasion*, my podcast co-host, author D. Harlan Wilson, joked with me saying, *"What good is teaching the formula if you don't use it?"* At that time, I was on the verge of the release of my 12th book, *The Last Night to Kill Nazis,* a WW2 vampire novel that would become my first national release. So, since I am confident in my writing ability, and because of my six-year immersion into the work and life of PKD, I felt that I was uniquely positioned to take Wilson's advice and begin to write a novel with Phil's formula.

I upped the ante on this project by deciding that I would essentially become a method actor in this novel. I was going to *try* to write this novel by imagining what it would be like if the guy who wrote this letter in the mid-60s—Philip K. Dick—was somehow transported to 2023. I wanted to try to imagine what Phil would think after spending a few months in our world. What came out of that experiment was a novel about the dangers of climate change, MAGA, the modern media, and, of course, social media.

One friend and writer I respect, Cody Goodfellow, questioned me about this project, asking who the fuck was I to do this? Honestly, I can understand why he thought I was acting from hubris. Another writer suggested that I couldn't write this without doing drugs, which, to me, was a bullshit claim since Phil wrote two masterpieces (A Scanner Darkly, VALIS) in the last few years of his life clean and sober.

Simply put, *Great America in Dead World* is an experiment. Ultimately, I sat down to write the novel utilizing my studies and immersion into PKD, often thinking, "What Would Phil Do?" and wondering, "How would Phil view this modern thing?" all while applying everything to Phil's formula.

I will confess, there were moments when I was writing more in my own voice, and yet there were other moments I would write something and laugh out loud because I unconsciously wrote something so Phildickian that it made me smile. To be honest, some of the political satire in this novel was, at times, more on the nose than Phil liked to write, and there are several sections here that I consider more John Brunner-influenced than anything else. But, overall, this is the novel that I feel like Phil might have written if he had travelled to 2023.

The theme of a warming world is one Phil explored quite often in his novels, and his major themes of his career—from what is human and what is reality to the class-imbalanced dystopia—are key to the narrative here. But, that is not all I did to pay homage to Phil. Some of the stylistic choices are intentionally out of date. For example, the science fiction novel *The Divine Invasion,* which Phil wrote in 1980, could have been written in the 60s. In other words, Phil did not attempt to modernize his science fiction. Calling cars "Autos" is one example of this, and naming the mouse-like inner eye internet control a "Ganglion" is also something I think Phil might do. But not necessarily something I would ever do.

The thin line between homage and when I asserted my own voice is best explained in a moment from Chapter 7 when Kai and Nick have a conversation about the philosophers Heidegger and Binswanger, which is something I would never do. At the same time, the author I am trying to homage here probably wouldn't have written the dialogue so bluntly as "Heidegger was a fucking Nazi." Also, in the club scene found in Chapter 9, I did not attempt to make it sound like a 60s author wrote it since I decided to include references to actual songs from the 80s, 90s and our modern day.

Phil's Formula Revealed

Let's talk directly about Phil's Formula and how I wrote this novel. Phil often wrote in the formula by instinct whereas I did outline this book heavily.

According to Phil's letter, the first thing to consider is the characters:

> *"Ch 1. First character, not protagonist but <<subhuman,>> that is, less than life. A sort of everyman who exists throughout the book but it is, well, passive, we learn the entire world or background as we see it acting on him; he is <<the guy who has to pick up the tab,>>the <<Mister Taxpayer>> etc. Okay. Dramatically we get little him, but, more important we see the world we are going to be inhabiting."*

Our "subhuman character" is Kai Dame, to the point that her body is heavily modified, and she is not considered fully human. As Phil suggests, the first chapter is an exercise in using the subhuman character to highlight the world-building. Kai can't afford to manipulate her dreams and she has to put up with constant ads. She also needs to have her avatar run her video game campaign to try and live in the GA+ simulation, and that is one way we learn about the world of *Great America*.

In a genre that is often centered around hot-shot pilots, generals, or the world's greatest scientists, Philip K. Dick is known for his working-class characters. Their lower status is portrayed when we read that they cannot afford to buy a real animal, or that they're unemployed pot healers looking for work. This is how Phil does world-building with minimal info-dumps.

On the last page of the letter, Phil makes an important note about these characters that seems to contradict his own subhuman label:

"Mr. G., small as he is, must never be made the victim of cruel lampooning by the author. Everyman may be small, but he must not be degraded, or the book becomes mere satire, mere spleen, this an error that even Pohl and Kornluth fell into from time to time."

Kai is a subhuman character, by Phil's definition. She is, however, never lampooned. My hope is the reader will be interested in her journey and keep reading. The next step in the formula is also character-based:

Ch ii. The Protag. Here he is. Mr.(as Bob Gilbert would say) Stonecypher; The character with the two-syllable name (as contrast the subhuman in ch I, who is named Al Glunch some unlikely short type name. What in reality the phonebook is full of...and for good reason; this is the <<other half>> of the world). Ah. Tom Stonecypher. He works for—and here comes the institute or organization or business..."

In the second chapter of *Great America in Dead World,* we meet President Supreme's Chief of Staff, Roger Greenstone. I think of him as Phil's two-syllable character and less of a Protag. I gave him a stone name as a tip of the hat to the formula. This character is the reverse of the subhuman, who is powerful. In this case, someone who is working for President Supreme.

Phil doesn't mention the government when talking about chapter two characters, but these characters are often officials within the bureaucracy; generally powerful, or in the case of Rick Deckard of *Do Androids Dream of Electric Sheep,* not powerful but making his money by working for the government. The examples of this sort of character are endless in Phil's novels.

Exceptions to the Rule

If you look at Phil's novels closely, you will notice how, at times, he will flip the order of the introduction of these character archetypes between chapters one and two. Both *UBIK* and *DADOES* flip the formula and introduce the "Protag" first and the subhuman characters second. The formula is not exact. In *UBIK,* for example, Joe Chip is less subhuman as he is "Mister Taxpayer" and is not introduced until Chapter 3.

It's also interesting to note that, in the outline, Joe was first named Joe Chippenfield, and Phil labeled him as the Protag, but as the story shifted to a primary focus on the secondary theme, his role changed. Phil, keeping with his formula, shortened the subhuman character's name to Chip.

> *"Ch iii Now. We switch tracks, and begin to develop in a manner forbidden to a short piece. We continue with both Mr. S and the subhuman Mr. Gulch… in a sense. But in another sense, although technically we carry on with Mr. S, we are in another dimension; that of the superhuman. This is the huge "they" problem, for instance, an invasion of earth, another sentient race, etc. and through Mister S's eyes and ears, we glimpse for the first time this superhuman reality."*

In Phil's formula, Chapter 3 is when the characters come together and the plot moves forward. In the context of *Great America in Dead World*, this is when Greenstone from Chapter 2 hires Kai, our subhuman character from Chapter 1. This fuse point is important for how the novel drives forward. Greenstone has a motivation that ties together with Kai.

Without seeing Phil's formula letter, researcher and author Patricia S. Warrick identified this trend in her 1983 essay "*Taoism and Fascism in High*

Castle." In that article, she talks about what she calls Dick's narrative technique and how it affects the three acts of his novels:

> *"In the first five chapters, the transient balance of each central character is disturbed. All movements are connected, often not directly, but the vibrations of an event occurring in one part of the narrative network will be felt by all."*

In the letter to Goulart, Phil spends two and a half pages explaining how he builds details about the characters. If you read *Great America In Dead World* closely, you can see all the ways that Phil wrote characters being used:

> *"...and so in a sense at the latter part of the book the two worlds or problems or dramatic lines fuse...This encounter of the Atlas domain with the personal problem of Mr. S. is the summa of the book because the long-maintained division between the vast They problem and the purely personal Mr.S problem has ended; the book all at once achieves a unity, the threads form one Gestalt."*

Each of Phil's novels using the formula has personal and world-sized problems, and three major themes that he meant to cover for each book. In my book, both Kai and Roger have personal problems that fuse them together. Kai needs money to join the Great America Sim. The way she wants to do that is by taking the job to convince Greenstone's father-in-law to give up his body and live as a brain in a box. Roger needs to get his "Heaven" brain box retirement. Their personal level problems fuse. The world-sized problem is the crash of the Foodle production and the fact that America is finally dying. Kai does not realize that, even if she gets the GA+ membership, it will be too late. Phil's letter spends half of page three and all of page four talking about how this final dramatic development can be accomplished with the hilarious example of the earth being destroyed by "*Demolishing green pea Giants from Betelgeuse IV.*"

Three Levels and Two Themes

On the last page of his letter, Phil sums it up neatly:

> *"I'm not saying, <<This is how to write a book.>> I am saying <<This is how I write a book.>> The two propositions are rather a bit different; would you not say? Anyhow dearly beloved, this is how PKD gets 55,000 words (the adequate milage) out of his typewriter. By have [sic] 3 persons, 3 levels, 2 themes (one outer or world sized, the other the inner or individualized-sized with a melding all, then at last a humane note."*

Using this template, I spent a good part of three whole days charting 30 PKD novels using this formula. The final humane note in his novels ranges from Joe Fernwright finding a planet where he can heal pots (*Galactic Pot Healer*), to Pete Garden beating the Vugs in a game of bluff and freeing humans in *Game Players of Titan*, to the first couple of his novels from the 50s that seemed to always end with characters heading off to a new colony world.

The use of the three levels is clear in most novels, but using *The Man in the High Castle* as a primary example I find the three primary levels to be: Childan's Jewelry Story and *The Grasshopper* novel showing us that nothing is real, the acceptance of evil as a part of daily life, and, finally, that history cannot be trusted.

Within these three levels, we often have world-sized individual or personal problems. That balance is found in every novel. From broke characters who can't afford basic items, or who work at very hard, low-paying jobs, to people who have to deal directly with alien threats or an invasion of a fake reality.

As I attempted to follow this formula, there was an interesting point where I needed to develop an ending and include the humane act at the end. One thing people often complain about with PKD's endings is that they often include codas that are twenty pages and seem to come out of nowhere. Sometimes, Phil recycled ideas from his earlier short stories. At the time I was writing this novel, I was also working on a short story that was about how the right and left wings of the political landscape create their own realities. It seemed like a great metaphor to explore as the extremes on each side do seem to live in their own reality. To me, it seemed like a Philip K. Dick metaphor. Kai getting to live in her own reality felt like a humane act. My editor, Keith Giles, correctly pointed out when he read the first draft, that this came a bit out of nowhere and suggested I fix it. Of course, I didn't. This was a feature, not a bug. Thankfully, Keith is also a serious Dickhead, so he understood as soon as we talked it through.

When I studied Phil's formula, I used this form below and filled it out based on 30 of his novels:

Two Persons:

Ch. 1: Subhuman/ Everyman:
Ch. 2 The Protag (who works for a Company or the Government)
Ch. 3 Combine and introduce the problem

Three levels:

2 Themes:

World Sized:

Individual-sized:

"And so in a sense, at the latter part of the book, the two world's problems or dramatic lines fuse"

Fuse point:

Getting Started

So, the first thing I did was to outline this project and take these ideas and apply them to this form. At the earliest state, this was all just an idea in my head.

Title: Great America in Dead World

Characters:

Chap 1: Subhuman: Kai Dame works as a "Janie"—Lower-class workers who support bio functions of the rich who live in the Great America simulation. The ecology is so bad Janies are augmented to survive. Anyone who is 50-P (more than half tech) is not considered fully human and have no rights.

Chap 2: The Protag, Roger Greenstone, Chief of Staff for President Supreme.

Chap 3: Kai is hired to support Roger's Philosophy professor and Father-In-Law who is refusing the upgrade to the gold plan (Heaven simulation).

The Three Story Levels:

Unlivable heat, spreading hunger and mass shootings, Fake realities, What is human?

The 2 Themes: MAGA to the endgame, life online.

World-Sized: The global temps are so high, Foodle crops are failing; the human race is dying.

Individual-Sized: Kai needs money to live online; she needs to convince Roger's Father-in-Law, Nick, to upload himself to Heaven.

Fuse Point: Kai takes Nick to DC, visits Congress and discovers right and left political parties separated into different dimensions.

Humane Act: Kai is allowed to leave her dying reality and hide in the progressive reality.

After I wrote this, I started my outline. My outlines are always chapter-by-chapter, but sometimes as short as a sentence. This project was different. I wrote a very detailed outline while trying to think of all the elements I wanted to hit. When I sat down to write, I would scan my outline once, and then start writing.

I can give you a warts-and-all example of Chapter 1:

Chapter I > Kai Dame's bed tells her it is time for work, she is awake, checking messages, and playing a game with her avatar. She doesn't have money for the next level of the game. Her AI is frustrated. The AI is supposed to go into sleep mode when she is online, but it doesn't. With her lack of money and concern for the game. She is confused when her avatar seems upset with Kai for paying for the Bathroom instead of skin for the game. She has the lowest access, which plays targeted ads for the game on her bathroom mirror. It includes a Weather and Shooting forecast. She is 40% biological. She needs the bathroom. Avatar doesn't understand. * Takes sky train to LA bubble district, re-routed for Foodle riots. Boss (Hank Hollis) assigns her a housing unit in the hills, a private home. Looking for a co-worker. She went to heaven, "and not the free one." (Folks selling Sauce, she needs it to keep wetware working)* Kai Cleans the disgusting pod, and talks to the client online through an avatar, as soon as she melts the Foodle into paste and injects the tube, she gets paid and the avatar goes to next level of the game. Kai is surprised. She wanted to play that level herself. We are introduced to Great America—the Sim world that people of means live in. Janies are a part of the support class who live in the climate-change-wrecked future. Their augments help them survive.

You can see that I followed the outline most of the time, but it is not one-to-one. Some nods to PKD: The Senator that helps Kai is named Hank Hollis (Herb Hollis was PKD's one and only boss at the record store, although I made a joke out of the name in the coda). I cut some things like Sauce and I didn't explain it for a few chapters.

The message of this novel is very important to me, but I suspect the fight against oligarchy and fascism is lost. I hope I am wrong, but I believe in the power of science fiction as a tool to talk about these issues. Just think of the Berkeley class of 1947 and the fiction of Ursula K LeGuin and Philip K. Dick who were both nominated for the all the major awards of the genre the year I was born. We can learn from them.

We are also very lucky that Philip K. Dick left behind a map of his formula. My hope is that others will continue to catch Phil's pink beam and surf it into other universes.

Book Club Study Guide

In the first chapter, the world-building is done through Kai. What elements of Kai's life informed you most about this world?

Philip K. Dick often recycled names from novels or stories he didn't expect to get published, like Pris in *We Can Build You* which was used again in *Do Androids Dream of Electric Sheep*. The Runcible characters in this novel are an easter egg from the outline for *Anti-Talent*, the novel that morphed into *UBIK*. The name in *UBIK* was changed to Runciter, however last name was used in a novel written before UBIK. Which novel?

In Chapter Three, there is a reference to juvenile class drones. In what 1950s SF novel did PKD have a surveillance system called "Juveniles"?

That constant battering of storms in DC is a homage to *Stormland* a recent Cli-Fi novel from cyberpunk legend John Shirley. He published a novel in 1978 that prompted William Gibson to call him "cyberpunk patient zero." What novel was that?

In Chapter Six, Roger Greenstone goes to meet Stephen Baxterman when he is about to have his brain boxed and his body composted. While Baxterman is a little less loathsome, he is based on a right-wing grifter and podcaster. Which one do you think he is inspired by?

In Chapter Seven, Kai begins to question if her Aver is living a secret life online. Not a super original idea, but one we think would have made Phil curious. In what ways does her Aver's activity make Kai feel paranoid?

In Chapter Nine, the video games Kai mentions playing for money are called "Night Warrior" and "Citizen Savior." How do you feel the game comments on right-wing culture?

In Chapter Ten, Nick and Miranda use their 24-hour trials of "Heaven for the Living" and both forget they are in Sim. Could you choose to live in a simulation if it were that realistic?

In Chapter Thirteen, Nick and Kai argue about philosophy. Nick can't shake the idea that, if they could make that virtual reality convincing, then why couldn't this one be engineered? What are your thoughts about simulation theory?

In Chapter Fourteen, Roger is suddenly pushing harder to enter the Heaven simulation. What is motivating him?

In Chapter Sixteen, the concept of Sunken Villages is mentioned. This is the idea that, since the working class can no longer afford to buy cars, all the underground garages of these massive towers have become living spaces. Many large cities are building massive housing towers that no one can afford to live in—or wants to. Does your community have a housing shortage? How is your community trying to deal with housing shortages?

In Chapter Twenty-One, Kayleigh Miller says "Kai, it is time you see that war, every single war that is declared or undeclared is for reality itself. Words kill more than bombs. Our side has prisoners, and they call them hostages. We have operations and they say it is an attack." Discuss with the group three ways in which governments or corporations rename acts of violence.

In Chapter Twenty-One, PKD often added codas that felt like they came from nowhere. I wanted this reveal to have that feeling, but seeds for it were planted throughout the novel. This chapter plays with the idea of realizing the "Great Separation" most Americans feel about our reality. Right-wing and Left-wing people often feel like they are not even in the same universe. Do you ever feel this way?

Glossary

A

Avers—Slang term for AI-generated Avatars that can perform in Video games for you when you sleep or at work.

Auto-Autos—Self-driving car/boat hybrids.

Aug-Hop—Music that plays directly inside body augmentation technology.

B

Brain-Boxes—The boxes that keep removed brains alive while in Heaven sim.

Brain-Boxing—Another name for The Great Upload.

Boxing Ceremony—The last rites before your body is composted and your brain is transferred to the heaven simulation.

Ballistocardiograms—Sleep sensors inside the dream circuit.

Blipp—To send electronic information from one person's server to another.

C

Cephalochromescope—Video quality recording of sim.

Citizen Savior—Online game where users fight mass shooters.

Chasers—Pop-up ad drones that follow you in the real world and pick up speed as you do.

Coins—Online game money that can be exchanged for cash and credit.

CoffeeISH—Almond-based coffee drink.

Conapts—This term is used throughout all PKD novels after the 60s to refer to an apartment building. Had to use it.

Convaid—AI text generator that suggests real-time conversation responses.

Coolant Tats—Tattoos that cool the skin.

D

Dermal Coolant Tabs—Under-skin cooling discs that are surgically inserted to compensate for rising temperatures.

Dirtside—Slang term for the ground used by people who live mostly in towers.

Dream Circuit—Inspires designer dreams, and sometimes features ads. Linked to a Smart bed that uses your weight to calculate how much you owe for Smart bed use.

Dust-Offs—Large dust storms.

E

Encephalscan—A brain scan.

Encelphalatraffic—Sim/Brain signal traffic interface.

Ear-Pal—An Aug that is implanted in your ear, AKA Cochleartron

F

Friend-Feed—Social network platform

Friendlies Pod Maintenance—Kai's Janie service.

Flurk - A random curse word.

Foodle—Protein paste made from Taro and Amaranth that provides protein, as very few products can grow in the future. There is one company that claims to make Almond-based Foodle.

Foodle-rhea—The food waste that drains from long-term life pods.

G

GA+—The Great American Plus online simulation.

Ganglions—Augments in the inner eye that control the inner eye net access menu. See also "Optical Sim control."

Ganglion hooks—Menu tabs that link to the net that can be seen in the inner eye.

Game Armor—Armor you can buy inside video games.

Great Upload—Another name for Brain Boxing.

Gogs—Smart goggles that people wear during dust-offs.

H

Heaven for the Living—Gold-level, life-like simulation system that requires Brain Boxing and composting of your body.

Heaveneers—Slang for Brain-Boxed people who choose to Sim in Heaven forever.

Hotbox—Slang for ground-level life. "Going to the hotbox." See also "Dirt-side."

Human percentage—Techies have a percentage of their body that is natural versus technological. For example, 50-P or 75-P. Many consider anyone with 50% technology augmentations as not human.

Hubrizine - Brain Box fluid that regulates brain activity.

HyperTube—A tunnel train that services the East Coast.

I

Insta—Late 21st century evolution of Instagram.

Ident-files—Searchable net-based identity search. Similar to Ident-Papes in PKD novels.

I.M.C implants—Internal moisture cycles, (sweat gland Augs for toddlers).

J

Janies—The slang term for the maintenance workers who maintain the life pods of people who live most of their lives in the Great America Plus sim.

K

Kibble—Cypto-currency that exists entirely online. A certain amount matches a real-life gold coin.

Kibble and Coin—A common saying. Like working for a living. i.e. "I am busting my ass for Kibble and Coin."

L

Lone Wolf Forecast—NRA-sponsored mass shooter prediction program.

Lib-Tards—Slang for boogeyman liberals; useful for blaming anything negative in society after the post-Second Revolution.

Life-Pods—Machines that help keep the bodies of those living in Sim alive.

M

Manager—The AI operating system on future versions of smartphones. Like a techno-control interface. It is designed to learn about you and operate everything in your life.

Moment-Reels—Photo scrolls you can share on social networks.

Museum of Human Experience—A place where GA+ users can visit to remember experiences that were unique to the real world.

N

Neighborhub—a social network.

Nats—Slang term from people with little-to-no tech augments. i.e. "Naturals".

Night Warrior—A popular video game based on eliminating mass shooters. The game accesses the historical details of over 100,000 available mass shooter events from the United States and Great American databases.

O

Optical Sim Control—See "Ganglion".

P

Phantoms—The slang term for people who are 70-P and controlled by their online self or others in the real world.

Polyencephalic Fusion—Communal Simming in Heaven for the living. GA Plus always runs at various speeds and is never a perfect fusion.

Pizzled—Tripping on drugs.

Protophasic Simulation Ports—Homes you buy inside Sim-worlds.

Pluggers—Floating ad drones that play targeted ads. See also "Chasers."

R

Rights Threshold—The percentage of technology to biology (49.9-P) where rights were lost under the American legal system.

Robotacops—Machine law enforcement drones in humanoid or four-legged versions.

S

Sauce—(Also known as 6-00-6). This drug was created for regulating body temperatures in heatwaves. Natural humans barely feel the effects, but Augments and cyborgs are treated to a brief, but powerful euphoria and experience less pain when interfacing with mechanical and biological joint intermixing. Sauce helps with the wetware interface. For techies, it is highly addictive. Example: *"She had a friend who kept $100 jars of Sauce in his fridge. He had nothing but Foodle smoothies and 6-00-6. His place was known to teenage techies as the Sauce Shack."*

Simmer (Simmy)—Slang for people who live most of their life online in GA+

Simmy-Sitters—Slang for Janies who monitor people's vitals while in simulation. Also used to refer to signal squatters.

Simwrecked—Slang for people stuck in a simulation

Sim-Skin—Another term for GA + Avers.

Sim-Cation—An entirely virtual vacation.

Second Revolution—The takeover of the government by the Conservative Party.

Smart Bed—50-P augments are charged for everything, including the use of their beds.

Snappy-Shot—Fireman delivery service.

Snatch_22—Popular gamer.

SkyMetro—O.C. Transit.

SkyTrams—Commuter trains and flying buses that circle above LA.

SkyTram Ports—Bus stops or traffic hubs built on top of skyscrapers.

Support Class—The Janies, farmers, and other lower class of people who have to live in the real world.

Stickparks—Parks lifted to cooler air.

Sunken Villages—Homeless camps built in old parking lots.

Stand-Ins—Fake, heat-resistant trees.

T

Techies—Slang for people who are 50-P or more.

Ten-Coin Tip—Automatic tips that deposit coins in games.

V

Videoport—Social streamer for short videos.

Videoframes—Picture displays that flip through a catalog of photos.

W

Wait Bot—Server droids inside the GA+ Sim. Some are robotic-looking, some are human-looking digital creations.

Numerical References

50-P—Anyone with more than 50 percent technology augments.

70-P—Anyone with more than 70 percent Tech.

300 Level Pro—A level of success in online games that unlocks money and rights for players.

About the Author

David Agranoff is a novelist, screenwriter, and Horror and Science Fiction critic. He is the twice-nominated Wonderland and Splatterpunk book award author of 12 books including the WW2 vampire novel, *The Last Night to Kill Nazis* (CLASH), the science fiction novel, *Goddamn Killing Machines* (CLASH) the Cli-Fi novel *Ring of Fire* (Deadite Press), *People's Park* (Quoir), and *Punk Rock Ghost Story* (Deadite Press). He is co-author of the novel *Nightmare City* (Grand Mal Press), with Anthony Trevino, which he likes to pitch as "*The Wire* if Clive Barker and Philip K Dick were on the writing staff."

He has written more than a thousand book reviews on his blog *Postcards from A Dying World,* which has recently become a podcast featuring interviews with award-winning and bestselling authors such as Stephen Graham Jones, Paul Tremblay, Alma Katsu, and Josh Malerman.

For the last seven years, David has co-hosted *The Dickheads* podcast, a deep-dive into the work of Philip K. Dick, reviewing his novels in publication order as well as covering the history of Science Fiction. His non-fiction essays have appeared on Tor.com, NeoText, and Cemetery Dance. He writes a regular column for *Amazing Stories* called 25th Century Five and Dime.

He just completed writing the book, *Unfinished PKD* on the fragments and outlines of Philip K. Dick's unpublished novels. David lives in San Diego, where he eats vegan pancakes, plays pickup basketball, and prepares to grow old in dead world.

To contact David Agranoff for speaking engagements,
please visit davidagranoff.blogspot.com
or @dagranoffauthor on X.

Many Voices. One Message.

quoir.com.